CONCERN FOR THE NERVOUS DISPOSITION OF WHIPPETS

ADRIAN BENTLEY

First Edition: July 2019

For Jéanine

PROLOGUE

"Shit! Let's move," said Nate, trying and failing to keep the panic from his voice.

He wrestled the helmet from the handlebars and moved it towards his head.

"Chill," said Charlie. "We'll just explain we're lost."

"We're in the middle of the friggin' desert."

"Okay, very lost."

Charlie stepped from his Harley and propped it on its kickstand.

"We need to get out of here," said Nate.

"It will be fine," countered Charlie.

The lights were getting closer and closer, bouncing as they reflected across the baked sand. In the distance, armed soldiers could be seen, silhouetted against the towering blaze, moving frantically, readying to attack. The sound of the jeep's engine grew louder and louder. Too close now, too late to flee. Within seconds, the jeep was upon them. It skidded to a halt and the engine died, the noise replaced by the angry Arabic shouted by the driver.

The soldier jumped out of the jeep, and Nate dropped the helmet and raised his hands to show he was no threat.

The soldier strode towards them. Nate watched as Charlie, arms raised, took a step forward.

"Tourists," said Charlie, smiling at the soldier.

Nate moved to get off his bike, but as he did so, he saw the soldier reach into his belt and pull a pistol from its holster. The soldier raised the gun quickly, the action followed by a loud crack. Charlie crumpled to the ground, and in that moment, Nate's brain checked out. Logic and reason disappeared, and paralysis took hold. He felt as though he were waking from a nightmare, lost in the first moments where the line between horror and reality was still being sought.

The soldier was still yammering, but Nate could hear no sound other than his own breath. The soldier raised the pistol towards Nate. The logical part of his brain told him he should flee, but he remained frozen in position, straddled across a Harley.

Nate waited for the pain to hit. But there was no crack of gunfire. Instead the gunman looked at his weapon in confusion.

And then the soldier appeared to be closer, very close, so close it didn't make sense. It took another fraction of a second for Nate to realise that it was not the soldier that was moving but him. The survival part of his brain, so used to being the passenger, had asserted authority and decided to get the hell out of there. The soldier took aim once more, but the bike struck him heavily and the gun flew from his palm.

The moment the soldier hit the ground, Nate's senses returned with a vengeance. The bike roared. The vibrations surged through his body, and he struggled to keep the Harley upright, accelerating farther away from his friend. He hated leaving him, but he knew Charlie was dead. Had been from the moment the bullet had ripped through his head. He now knew which part of the nightmare was real—all of it.

Nate sped over the bumpy sand until he was back on the road. He turned right at the tarmac, heading back towards Marsa Matrouh.

He looked to see if he was being pursued, but except for the light far off in the distance, the desert was dark. It was that light that had beckoned them away from the road in the first place, a decision that had changed his life and ended the life of his best friend.

He noticed that his vision was blurry, and only then did he realise he was sobbing.

And then he heard a noise echoing through the desert, a sound that chilled his heart. He turned and saw lights in the sky moving towards him quickly. Two helicopters. He accelerated the bike as fast as it would go, but it wasn't fast enough. The noise of the blades cut through the air, louder and louder. Suddenly the world turned white as a blinding light shone down from above, as if God himself were summoning him. There was no way out. Nate was going to die.

And that's when he thought of Sally. The woman he loved and whose face he knew he would never see again. He had been an idiot, and now he knew he would never be able to make it right.

As Nate sped through the desert, he knew he was going to die alone.

ONE

Hope lay dead on the linoleum, its body prostrate and bloody. Hope had flown in through the window only eight months earlier, when Alison and David had started the business. Quickly realising this was not an environment where it could prosper, Hope had made a sharp exit towards the window, where it had struck the pane headfirst, and then, like a disorientated fly, instantly tried again with similar results. As the weeks went by and the business failed to take off, Hope's escape attempts became more frantic. Many times it looked towards Alison and besieged her with its eyes for release, but Alison never did. Maybe it was because deep down she wanted it here, but mostly it was that Hope was a metaphorical construct, and as such, invisible.

Hope had died the moment Alison opened the letter. The hug that followed was instant and unexpected. It had collapsed on her like an avalanche—albeit an avalanche where the snow had been replaced by the upper torso of a six-foot black man named David. It wasn't the first time that he had hugged her, far from it. It was just that in the past there had been a certain degree of warning that had accompanied the action.

"You're hugging me," said Alison. "Why are you hugging me?"

"I thought you were going to cry."

"Oh," replied Alison, after giving the issue some thought.

"Do you want me to stop?"

"Nope, it's fine."

They remained like this for another few seconds.

"Is it getting weird?" asked David.

Alison considered the question for a little while, then said, "A little."

David released Alison from the hug.

Newly free from the hugalanche, Alison smiled sadly.

"It's not so bad. We can find another sponsor," said David.

"There's no one," said Alison. "We now have no money coming in. Yesterday we didn't have anywhere near enough money coming in. Yesterday seems like a golden age now."

The sponsorship from Nathanson's had kept them afloat over the past weeks. When everyone else had pulled their funds, they had stayed. The money had not been huge; they were still operating at a loss, but with the remains of Alison's redundancy payment and the small amount of money David pulled in from acting work, it had been enough to keep going.

They had continued on the basis that a corner would be turned, but unfortunately there had been none, and the road had run straight and downward.

"And tomorrow?" asked David.

Alison shrugged. "It's too late to get the money back. Let's go. Maybe it will give us an idea for the next project."

"Next project? Another magazine?" questioned David.

"Maybe. Maybe something else. It's possible, isn't it?"

David nodded. "More than possible but…"

"I can try for temping work to get some money," said Alison, the determination taking hold in her voice.

"I have a better idea," said David, making a sudden flourish with his hands. "We need money and…" He pulled his hands apart to reveal a five-pound note between his fingers.

"You are such a nerd. And anyway, that trick stops being impressive after the first hundred or so times."

"I'll have you know, I am a professional magician."

"You were a magician's assistant - for a month."

"They're pretty much the same thing."

"I think the Magic Circle would care to differ."

Alison knew the trick wasn't meant to impress her. It was meant to make her smile, and once again, it had worked. David was a man who always knew what was needed in any situation. People still thought they were a couple. Maybe it was the amount of time they spent together. But Alison and David were not a couple. That hope had lasted all of about ten minutes - or to be precise, the length of time between first

11

meeting him and seeing the look on his face when a strapping rugby player had walked into the student union. The truth, though, was that Alison's friendship with David had survived far longer than any of her romantic relationships.

"About tomorrow," said David, a look of apology sweeping across his face.

"What about it?"

"I have an audition at nine. I'll be with you by eleven, promise."

"The audition? Shakespeare? Chekhov?"

"Johnson. Actually, Johnson & Johnson. They may have been brothers."

"It can't be for shampoo - you're bald."

"Shaved! A shaved head is a lifestyle choice; baldness isn't. It's for toothpaste."

Alison's mobile vibrated, and she looked at the screen. There was a new email. The sender's name seemed familiar. She tapped the screen and read the contents.

And over in the corner, the creature on the linoleum twitched.

. . .

The lift doors opened, and Alison and David walked into the corridor, instantly hit by the smell of fresh carpet. It was a corridor that looked distinctly un-lived in. Numerous abstract framed prints had been placed along the walls to try to give some sense of a home, but in doing so simply showed the anonymous nature of the building. To Alison it resembled a reasonable hotel, plush, with all necessary conveniences, but she couldn't imagine living here.

There was a series of distant bangs, and Alison felt the corresponding vibrations through the thick carpet.

The corridor stretched out in front of them. Ten cream-coloured identical doors.

"You don't think this is actually going to lead to anything, do you?" asked David. "We aren't the first here. Pretty much every red top reported on the story."

"But the people at the red tops don't have our journalistic integrity," said Alison.

David smiled. "Yes, I'm sure they are all very worried about us. I mean, who wouldn't be? Woodward and Bernstein, mere amateurs."

"Sometimes I think you lack the correct attitude," said Alison.

They walked down to the end of the corridor, counting down the numbers on the doors until they reached their destination.

"Have you noticed the cameras?" asked Alison.

David looked around.

Alison continued. "There was one on the ceiling of the lobby and two on this floor. That's high security for a residential building. What are they keeping in this place?"

"Maybe it's that," said David, pointing to one of the paintings.

At the end of the corridor was a very different painting to the rest of the bland abstracts. It was a study in demons and mutilation, like a landscape of Hell. Alison had never studied art, but she knew the same famous artists as everyone else, and she recognised the style of the painting rather than the work itself.

"I think it's a Hieronymus Bosch," said Alison.

"It's a bit out of place, isn't it?"

Alison turned and looked at the door that faced the painting. The chrome numbering on the door read 342.

"That's the flat."

Alison suddenly had second thoughts about the whole thing. "It's worth checking out, isn't it? Even if nobody else thought there was anything to report?"

"It wasn't that they didn't think there was anything to report. It was just what they reported probably wasn't what he wanted as a legacy."

Alison took a moment to weigh it up. Could they do anything other than cause further grief to the widow? But it was the widow who had asked them to come. Alison pressed the doorbell and heard it chime inside.

"He was a great reporter. That should be his legacy."

From the other side of the door, movement could be heard, and then the sound of a chain being pulled back.

The door was opened by a dark-haired woman in her early 30s, her eyes red from crying. This was the woman Alison had seen in the papers that had reported on Colin Trent's death.

She felt sorry for her. It must be hard enough losing somebody without the ridicule that had rained down on both of them due to the circumstances of his demise.

"Mrs Trent?" asked Alison, more quietly than she intended.

The woman behind the door nodded.

"Please call me Isabella." She forced a smile. "You must be from the magazine," she said with a soft but distinct Eastern European accent. She opened the door fully. "Come in."

The flat was sparsely decorated. No pictures on the walls, no trinkets or ornaments, nothing to differentiate it from an "off the shelf" show home set to its default setting.

"Thank you for coming. Please take a seat." She pointed to a leather sofa.

Alison and David sat down on the sofa, which squeaked beneath them as they sat.

"Do you still live here?" asked Alison. "I believe that you and Colin were divorced?"

Isabella smiled sadly. "I never lived here. Colin moved here when we separated. The sound of building work would have driven me insane." She took a seat in the armchair next to the sofa.

"I wondered what the banging was," said Alison.

"I think Colin liked it here. It reminded him of work. He was always happiest in war zones." The thought made her smile.

"You remained friends with your husband?" asked David.

"Life is complex. We were always great friends. He was

15

my soul mate. But life doesn't always work out as you might imagine."

"We were a bit confused as to why you contacted us. So much has been written about his death," said Alison.

"I did not ask you to report on his death. I asked you here to report on his murder."

Alison and David remained silent, surprised at the direction the conversation had taken. Every tabloid had covered the story, and not one of them had suggested there was anything suspicious about the death.

"You think your husband was murdered?" asked David.

"I know he was murdered."

"If that were the case, why did none of the other newspapers report this?" asked Alison.

"They did not report it because his murder is impossible."

Alison and David paused, waiting for Isabella to continue. In the end, David broke the silence.

"The papers said that your husband died from autoerotic asphyxiation."

"I know what the papers said. They were wrong. Everybody was wrong. The papers reported that Colin was found naked with a belt around his neck and pornography around his body. That was true; that's how I found him. But I know it was murder."

A silent question hung between Alison and David.

"I know it was murder," continued Isabella, "because the magazines were the wrong sort. The pictures were of naked

16

women. That was not what Colin liked." She reclined back in the chair.

"Are you saying that your husband was gay?" asked David.

Isabella nodded. "It was not widely known outside of his friends. Colin took his job very seriously. There are many countries in the world where it is difficult to report if one does not fit the accepted norms. Colin always believed that the more barbaric the country, the more reporting was needed. He didn't want to make his personal life an issue."

"You said that his murder was impossible?" asked Alison.

Isabella tried to reply, but her emotions overcame her.

"I'm sorry. We can come back later if you wish."

Isabella. shook her head. "No, stay, please. One moment."

Alison and David sat in silence until Alison gave in.

"Is there any tea in the kitchen?" she asked.

Isabella nodded, but before Alison could stand, David was on his feet and moving towards the kitchen. "I've got it," he said.

Realising on the way that he had neglected to obtain certain information, he turned. "Er, where do you keep the tea bags?"

"Cupboard closest to the sink. Cups are there, too."

The two women fell back into awkward silence. Alison could see that Isabella was failing in her battle to avoid tears. She reached out, enveloping Isabella's hand in hers, and then instantly questioned whether it was the right thing to do.

"I'm sorry," said Isabella.

"There's no need to apologise."

"He was a good man. He saved me." She paused, but before Alison could ask what she meant by the statement she continued. "I am Chechen. Colin was reporting there ten years ago. When he met me, I was in a bad place. My life was in danger. I needed to leave, but that was not possible. Colin helped me."

"He smuggled you out?"

"In manner of speaking. He married me."

"You knew he was gay?"

"Yes. I knew everything. It was a marriage of convenience. I married him to get out of there. He was a nice man, but I never expected such a close friendship with him. I loved him. But it could never be."

"You divorced him?"

Isabel shook her head sadly. "He divorced me. It was only supposed to be for a few years. He thought he was holding me back. He knew I wanted a family but realised I would never leave him. He understood I loved him."

"Who would want to murder him?" asked Alison.

"He was an investigative reporter. He had many enemies. Lots of people wanted him dead. And if he had been murdered in the street, shot through the head, everybody would be asking who did it. But they are not, are they? They are instead laughing. Those so-called journalists have none of the integrity or courage that he had. How much fun they had at his expense," she said, the bitterness in her voice now clear. "But if they are not going to stand up and ask questions, I must find somebody who will."

"You know we are not a big publication, yes? There may be other people better placed to look into this," said Alison.

Isabella nodded. "Big publications. They came, they looked, they found nothing. I need someone who will fight for Colin. I will fight as hard as I can. I will fight until the last breath I take. But in this, I will need help."

David returned with cups of tea, and talk resumed. Alison and David asked questions, Isabella answered. It was clear at the end of their conversation that, at least if what Isabella said was true, a murder was clearly impossible. Isabella gave Alison the number of the policeman in charge of the case at Scotland Yard, and Alison said she would contact him.

In truth, though, she wasn't expecting to get much support.

. . .

Alison and David waited behind a plain wooden table. The interview room had walls of red brick and yellow fluorescent lighting. The place felt claustrophobic and intimidating.

They had been waiting for thirty minutes, and it was now approaching 6 p.m. When the smiling DC had shown them in, Alison couldn't help but feel there were those in the station who were amused by their presence. But maybe that was just her imagination.

"Did you notice anything strange when we walked in?" asked Alison.

19

"Like what?"

"Like how everyone was so nice."

"That's because we're awesome."

"Yeah, that would be it. It's just that our awesomeness has never had that effect on police officers before. Especially after 5 p.m. on a Friday."

"Honestly, this whole thing is a little strange."

"Maybe we should just go?" said Alison. "I would love to help Isabella out. I feel so sorry for her, but there is no mystery here. The whole world has looked at this death. They have pored over every pathetic little detail and found nothing but a sad tragedy. Then they took the piss."

Their conversation was interrupted by the door opening, and a tall, suited man entered. His face was bleak and humourless. He held an A5 manila envelope in his hand.

"Detective Inspector Nick Grant," he said. His greeting far from warm, like a little ray of darkness amongst beams of suspicious law enforcement light.

Without another word, Grant walked past the desk towards an ancient wheeled audio-visual unit that stood at the rear of the room. He dragged it, wheel casters squeaking, across the floor and positioned it directly opposite Alison and David.

"Thanks for meeting with us," said Alison. "We were hoping you could help us. We're looking into the death of Colin Trent."

Remaining silent, Grant pulled a DVD from the envelope and put it into the player on the shelf below the TV.

The TV crackled to life to reveal a screen divided into four equal frames. The images in three of the quadrants were black and white and grainy, but the lower-right quarter was in colour and of better quality.

Alison looked at David, who shrugged. Maybe Grant was simply a man of few words—or maybe he was just allergic to small talk.

"These are the four videos we have of the Trent property," said Grant.

"Have other people questioned the death?" asked Alison.

"If the widow has asked you to come here, then I know why. Trust me, we can all get this over with quickly if we just watch the videos."

He turned his attention back to the TV and continued. "The black-and-white images are from the building itself." He pointed to the first three images. "That one is from the reception, and the other two are from either end of the fourth floor."

Grant pointed at the screen and the black-and-white rendering of the doorway opposite the Bosch painting. "That is Colin Trent's flat. This recording covers the two days before Mr Trent's approximate time of death and continues until SOCO cleared the scene. I have watched every single frame of this very boring tape and can tell you that Colin Trent went into the flat on Saturday morning, and nobody else entered or exited the property until his wife showed up on Sunday to find him cold, naked, and hanging from his neck."

It was clear from his tone he felt that Alison and David were wasting his time. But Alison pressed on. "What is the fourth video?"

"Well, if nobody went in the door, the only other potential entry points are the windows. There are two of them, one for the bedroom, one for the living space and kitchen. This video shows them both. Mr Trent lived on the fourth floor, so entry this way would be challenging to say the least. This video shows it was impossible."

David sat forward and pointed at the colour image. "Where does this video come from?"

"Mr Trent had a complaining neighbour. There are not many people living in the building, but this neighbour owned the property opposite."

"He was filming Colin Trent's flat?" asked Alison.

"Not on purpose. He was filming that," said Grant, pointing to the lower two thirds of the frame, which showed the building site underneath Colin Trent's window. Alison watched the pixels move, picking up brief detail of the yellow jacketed workers as they walked around the site. "He seemed to believe that he could move into a building under construction and expect silence."

"And this man checks out?" asked David.

Grant nodded. "He's a very strange guy, with a long history of complaining. This was certainly not out of character. And before you ask, the video has been checked, and it hasn't been edited. That's the case for all the videos. What you see is what happened. They are really, really boring."

"Why were there so many cameras in Colin Trent's building?" asked David.

"The building was supposed to be completed six months ago, but renters seemed disinclined to move into a building that was unfinished. With most of the property being empty, they had some issues with squatters and thieves. Most of the pictures on the walls were stolen and replaced a number of times. In the end, both the building managers and residents agreed that it was in their interest to increase security."

Grant, seeing that another question was on its way, got in first. "Were you encouraged to come here today by my colleagues?"

"We would have come anyway," replied Alison. "But they were very friendly."

"I'm afraid people are wasting your time. For reasons I don't care to go into, I am not overly popular at the moment. People have been ordered to throw me every annoying job going. If there is a waste of time or a tedious piece of work to do, it ends up on my desk."

Grant hit the button on the DVD and ejected the disc. "You seem like nice people, so take my advice: Go home. Enjoy your weekend. There is no mystery here."

Alison needed more. "Do you know that Colin Trent was gay, and - " said Alison.

"The pornography found by him was straight," interrupted Grant. "I do. Maybe he was curious. I don't know. What I do know is that it is impossible that he was murdered. If I am wrong, then it would take someone with the genius of Moriarty to pull this off." He pointed to the TV. "Do you know why we have that in this room? It's because criminals are almost always idiots. They carry out crimes in full view of CCTV cameras. They do this because they're morons. Moriarty was a piece of literary fiction. In the real world, criminal geniuses don't exist."

TWO

It dawned on Spencer Townsend that he was a criminal genius at the exact moment he took the first sip of his cappuccino. He had been tested, and he had achieved the impossible. Colin Trent, the famous investigative journalist, had been murdered, and not even the most deluded conspiracy theorists thought there was anything awry. The secret that Spencer had been contracted to keep was intact, and what's more, the Emissary had told him that the Russian was pleased. Maybe now the Russian would see that it was counterproductive for Spencer to have two jobs. Surely his days at MI5 were numbered. It was time to stop walking the line. Spencer was comfortable with the dark side.

He took another sip, and in doing so caught sight of the sleeve of his cheap suit. Spencer was forty-five years old, and most of his life had been spent in cheap suits. When he joined

MI6 straight from university, he couldn't afford nice clothes, and even as he had climbed the ranks, the job by its very nature involved not standing out. His sartorial condition had improved not one ounce when he crossed the Thames to MI5.

Henry David Thoreau said that the mass of men led lives of quiet desperation. What he should have said was that they led lives of quiet desperation and polyester. The object of being a spy was to blend with the populace, to hide in plain sight. It took a level of self-discipline most of the populace simply didn't possess. Spencer had been restrained for twenty-five years. It was time to get compensation for his life of austerity. Soon he would be able to ditch the shoddy threads.

Spencer looked around. The day was sunny, and being lunchtime, the offices had begun to spill out, and the park was filling up with lovely young things. Spencer loved this time of year. If the sun was out, he would come to the café in St James whenever he was able. It wasn't just tulips that reacted well to warmth and sunlight. Suddenly women who'd rendered themselves invisible with bulky warm clothing for ten months of the year would show some skin and instantly bloom. Skirts had replaced trouser suits. Spencer liked skirts. He liked to think how little lay between him and that special place he would so like to stick his face.

But whilst the sunlight had lots of positives, it wasn't so good for Spencer, who was a man known to perspire. His mother said it was because he needed to lose weight, but what did that bitch know about exercise? She had wasted her life in front of the TV. Spencer had been around the world, protecting the country. She would never know this, of course. There was no way the loose-lipped idiot would be able to keep it to herself. He figured she would be the first piece of baggage to be jettisoned in his new life.

Spencer considered removing his jacket and hanging it over the back of the uncomfortable, overly small chair that only accommodated three quarters of his arse. He had made the unfortunate mistake of wearing a blue shirt, and he just knew the sweating under his arms was sure to be obvious. He didn't want to look bad in front of all the lovely things in the park. Spencer blamed the cheap suit for the way he sometimes sweated.

It was a discovery made when he had first worn bespoke suits. Unlike the cheap rubbish he was wearing now, those suits were made from top-quality material that breathed. The suits had been a gift from the Russian and had been arranged by the Emissary. The Emissary had even visited Spencer at his home. How the man had known where Spencer lived was a question that would need to be addressed at some point. The Emissary had been joined by a tailor. Spencer usually hated getting measured, always feeling that there was some element of judgement being made about his form. This man had been professional and respectful, though, and within twenty minutes, both men were gone, and twenty-four hours later the new suits were delivered.

The Emissary, despite being a very strange little man, had

so far proved highly resourceful. Spencer had almost laughed when the Russian had introduced them. At first he had put it down to the language barrier. Certainly the willowy, bespectacled man didn't look like anyone deserving a title of such respect. The man may have been softly spoken and appeared to have little gravitas, but he had been Spencer's only contact with the Russian except for that first meeting. Spencer had put together a shopping list of what was needed, and the man had delivered every time. He wished some of the Muppets in MI5 were as good.

Spencer's gaze fixed on a dark-haired beauty in a flowing white dress. Probably no more than twenty, she was sprawled on the grass, laughing with her friends. Even from this distance he could see her skin was immaculate. She had a glow.

Spencer realised he was hard. He moved his chair farther under the metal table, even though he was pretty sure no one could see. Maybe he would call the agency tonight. He knew he had to be careful. MI5 always took an interest in how their officers spent their home life. Fraternisation with common prostitutes would not be viewed with approval at Thames House. That said, the agency that he had used on the night of Trent's murder didn't employ common prostitutes.

It had been a stressful day, and Spencer had been unable to sleep. When his phone rang, he almost jumped out of his skin. Spencer had never been more nervous about answering a call in his life. He just knew that they had made a mistake and his life was over. But it was the Emissary on the other line.

Spencer came close to losing his temper at being contacted at that time of night, but the Emissary's quiet voice had calmed him. Spencer hadn't even baulked when the man referred to himself as "the Emissary", concluding this was only because it was the name Spencer knew. The Emissary said he was just phoning to check he was alright, but in hindsight it was almost as though he knew that Spencer needed to talk. The conversation had lasted only ten minutes, but by the end, Spencer felt confident that his operation had gone without fault. Just before hanging up, the Emissary had given him a number to ring and instructions to ask for Maria. When Spencer questioned further, the man hung up.

Spencer had phoned the number and given the name. Maria was waiting for his call, and within an hour she was at his door, dressed in a long flowing dress, dark hair surrounding spectacular green eyes, pale flawless skin. She was a vision. And at that moment Spencer questioned whether the Emissary could read minds, as the woman standing before him was Spencer's idea of perfection.

Now he realised why he was fixated by the woman in the park and why he was so unbelievably hard. It was because it took him back to that night. Spencer could remember her scent and her taste. Her English had been adequate, though spoken with an Eastern European accent that ordinarily he would have found annoying. Yet the things she had done to him that night had been incredible. The night had changed him. He knew that now. His vitality had been decimated by his time in the Service. He knew he had reached as far as he was going to get in MI5. His face didn't fit. He hadn't gone to Eton and Oxbridge like Holloway, the man who had stolen Spencer's last promotion from under his nose.

Fucking Holloway. He was so much better than Holloway, and Eddington before him. There was no way either of those losers could have pulled off what he had. They were A to B thinkers, lacking the level of imagination to pull off the perfect murder.

He was right to make the deal with the Russian. He knew that now. Unlike the Service, this was a man who could spot talent.

He had been depleted. But this new life that lay in front of him was so enticing that Spencer couldn't help but smile. He would throw away the cheap suits and move out of the small flat. Maybe he would take up running, lose a bit of weight. He looked across the park and wondered how much fanny could be his if he really applied himself.

With Trent dead, all he needed to do was to find the reporter's source. Spencer realised that his new job would mostly involve firefighting, and he was okay with that. The Egyptians had fucked up, but then what do you expect from Arabs? Now Spencer had to pick up the pieces. He wasn't worried. He had a handpicked team - a mix of youthful brutality and experience. The biker would be dead within the week, of that Spencer was sure.

Spencer had been thrilled to assemble his team. His main

man was former SAS. Chuck Banner had been the best of the best until a brutality charge was unfairly levelled at him. Spencer had known him from the field and knew him to be a well-trained man. And smart. He was a true artist. His art was killing, but that was why the country was paying him. He was the savage that kept them safe. But details of an "incident" had found their way into the press, and Banner was one of four who were let go.

As it turned out, being booted out of the forces had been the best thing that ever happened to him. Banner had become a soldier for hire, and he had a skill set that was in demand. Spencer had to make a large offer to get him back to England, but it had been a bargain. With Spencer still working at Thames House, it had been Banner, working with the Emissary, who had put the rest of the team together. When Spencer wasn't around - which would be most of the time - Banner would be the boss, and Spencer had no doubt that he would be able to handle any situation.

Banner had brought over five mercenaries he knew and trusted. One of them appeared to be a runt as far as Spencer could tell, but Banner said the man had a needed skill set, so Spencer had let it go - for the time being, at least. Banner had picked up the rest of the team from a list that Spencer had put together. These men were legends in the security services. Banner had questioned their ages, but Spencer knew that there was no substitute for experience. Anyway, he had Banner's mercs for the physical stuff.

The runt might need management, though. Spencer resolved to reflect on the man's employment in a week's time. Banner was adamant that the man was an asset, but as far as Spencer could make out, he was just a weedy Scouse spastic. He had met him when Spencer had gone to the hotel to introduce himself to his employees. They had a few drinks, and all was well until the runt spilled his beer on Spencer's new suit. The little runt apologised, but you could see he was laughing inside. He probably realised that the suit was worth more than his total belongings. Spencer had been calm. It wasn't good management to rant. Not yet.

The dark-haired woman stood up from the grass and headed back to work with her friends. Spencer looked at his watch. The hour had gone too quickly. He needed to get back to Thames House, and he hated the fact. He would need to give it a minute or two, though.

As Spencer waited for his erection to recede, he thought about the situation he was now in. He was the general to a private army. There was clearly no one that could stand in his way.

. . .

Alison drove her knee into the attacker's groin. The padding absorbed the impact, and thus, rather than being rendered into a crying mess on the floor, her assailant was able to retaliate with a punch towards her head. Alison sensed the movement, and her arm came up instinctively, deflecting the swing, which flew past her head with more than an inch to spare.

"Okay," cried a voice. Twenty leisure-wear-covered individuals stopped their attempt at controlled violence and looked at the instructor.

Alison put her hands to her knees and breathed deeply. She was out of breath but looked considerably less exhausted than the rest of the group. She remembered when she had first come to this class five years ago. How she had to stop after ten minutes, feeling that her lungs were liable to explode. She remembered waking up the next day and how her body had ached so much that she almost didn't return for a second lesson. She tried not to remember the event that had led her to come to the class in the first place, but she failed, as she always did.

Alison had taken up Krav Maga to protect herself, and in many ways it had been her saviour. These classes were always here for her when things were getting her down. There was nothing quite like beating up a middle-aged accountant to make you feel at peace with the world. Alison looked over at her opponent, who was sweating profusely. Never had a man been so grateful for the invention of cushioned kick pads.

Alison often wished that Krav Maga had some sporting applications or grading system to check her progress. Although, any sport that involved testicle punching and eye gouging as a general part of its methodology would probably not get past any medical board - and the bouts would be necessarily short.

Krav Maga had been developed by the Israeli Defense Forces and could - at least for those who couldn't see the beauty of the form - be described as the martial art of fighting really dirty. It was a form of power and strength and one where the absence of testicles could be a distinct advantage.

Alison waited for those around her to get their breath back. After a moment, the teacher told the group to begin punching practice. The accountant didn't look like he fancied being punched, but he picked up the large pad and placed it against his shoulder.

Her ability to defend herself was one of the few things in Alison's life that she had independently brought into existence. Up until a few hours ago, she'd had the magazine, but now that was gone, along with all her dreams of being a modern-day Nancy Drew.

It was possible for Alison to make her hobby her career. She had been asked by the instructor a couple of times to lead a class when she was on holiday, but she had always said no. This was her other life, and she didn't want to bring the stresses of work into this room. When she pounded groins, she was doing it for fun, not profit.

Alison's fist was starting to get sore, but she continued punching forward, maintaining her form and savagery. She thought about Isabella Trent and how heartbroken she had been. Alison hated herself for wishing there was a better story behind Isabella's tears, but there wasn't - there was just sadness.

THREE

Mattie Thomson had always wanted to kill. Almost every method of murder had been practiced over and over in his imagination. He just had never actually done it. Mattie was a murder virgin, and it was really beginning to weigh on his mind. And they knew it. Mattie's virginity was like a bad smell in this company, even though, in truth, he had been less than impressed by these so-called professionals.

The boss was a right twat, too. The fat pompous prick had already taken a dislike to Mattie. He could tell. Mattie could suss people instantly. It was like some kind of ESP that let him know when people didn't like him. As soon as he had met the boss, Mattie's ESP moron-o-meter had spiked. The guy was never going to give him a chance. Same as it ever was, Mattie thought to himself.

On the bright side, Mattie didn't think he was going to have to put up with the fat boss often. The man had turned up only once in the two weeks Mattie had been at the hotel. Mattie had spilled some of his drink on that occasion. He hadn't been drunk and never was or would be. He had seen what drink can do to people, and that wasn't something he wanted in his life. He had accepted a beer just to be part of the team.

All was going well until the obese bastard bumped Mattie's arm, and a few drops splashed from the bottle of Carlsberg over the tosspot's suit. It was just an accident, and everyone could see it, but the fat sod lost it. You would have thought someone had shit on his cat the way he reacted. He even called Mattie a spastic. That was a word his father had used to describe him, but that was decades ago. Mattie had looked the word up when he was younger and saw that it referred to people with a disability. He couldn't understand why his father had used the word because Mattie didn't have a disability, and it seemed to be an idiotic insult that showed that the user didn't care about ill kids, and that just made the insulter look like a tool. The once popular insult had faded out of fashion as Mattie progressed through school. Spastic was now the Hitler moustache of putdowns - and the fat bastard had used it. Ergo twat.

The guy obviously thought he was James Bond or something. At least Mattie didn't lie to himself. They were the bad guys, and Mattie was fine with that. Along with his ESP, he had a good moral compass. He couldn't help it if the moral compass had been set up just a bit differently from others. For Mattie,

36

North was South, just as wrong was right, and that suited him just fine. He understood that other people wanted to be like him. Wished they too lived with freedom from guilt. Mattie was bad to the bone. Bad to the bone. He liked that. Maybe he would get a tattoo with that written below a snake or a tiger, or a snake fighting a tiger - with a knife. Yeah, that would be cool as fuck.

Mattie looked towards his colleague. This really wasn't what he'd signed up for. He had been sitting in the back of a van with a geriatric git for the last six hours. It wouldn't have bothered him so much if the guy could speak English - or at least was prepared to speak English to him. Some crack unit this turned out to be - the majority of the team were proper ancient, like fifty or something.

They had been waiting outside some house for hours, and for what? So this cabbage-loving wrinkly could relive his youth? The house had been bugged for the past week. It was clear to any idiot that the residents had no idea where their son was, but still the Communists persisted.

The headphones were making Mattie's ears sweat. This was the third day of listening. It wouldn't have been so bad if most of it hadn't been boring as shit. Yes, they talked about their son. In fact, they did nothing but talk about him, on and on and on. God, it was dreadful. Occasionally they would cry. Even the father had cried, something that Mattie's father had never done. Mattie had even tried to make a joke of it, but the miserable fuck sitting next to him hadn't found it funny.

37

Commie motherfuckers just didn't understand humour. Mattie had seen pictures of Russia from ages ago. It looked properly bleak. All grey and snowy. Mattie wondered if it was this that made them all so miserable. Or maybe it was them all being miserable that had turned the country grey and bleak.

Chickens and eggs, thought Mattie.

Even when the exciting stuff did happen, Mattie wasn't allowed to go along. No, he had to stay in the van like some kind of dog. It was shite anyway. Banner had told him about it back at the house. It was called Zersetzung. Mattie had nodded as Banner explained it, but in truth he didn't really understand. It was all about stealth interrogation by disruption of the inner self - or some bollocks like that. It was all too complicated. Everyone knew that if you wanted to interrogate someone, you tied them naked to a chair and started cutting them until they gave up the information. That was textbook. Mattie so wanted to do that. He had mentioned it when the fat boss was around, but they had all just laughed at him.

That was when he'd first realised that the boss didn't like him. He had looked at Mattie, shook his head like he was addressing an unruly child, and out loud, said something about people having ideas above their station. What kind of management style was that? He should be encouraging open debate, not inviting the rest of the group to ridicule the only person in the room making sensible suggestions. And they had all laughed with him. Even the ones that refused to speak English, which just showed that they did understand the language and were just being rude. The fuckers.

And what had been the result of their Jedi skills of invisible interrogation? Fuck all, that's what. Hardly surprising, really, considering that it seemed to mostly involve breaking into the house at night and moving objects around. The Cabbage Muncher had even gone so far as sending the lady of the house a vibrator in the post. At which point it should have been clear that he was just a pervert who got off on creeping around houses while people slept. The commie bastard had got Mattie to buy the vibrator. Mattie had been the only bloke in Ann Summers. He'd bought a nine-inch dildo that day. The bloody thing was green. What the fuck was that about?

Banner had no time for this bollocks. Mattie could tell. It was down to his ESP again. Yes, Banner could see Mattie's potential. Banner was a talent spotter, and in Mattie he had seen a true protégé.

Mattie had met Banner in a war zone in West Africa. Banner was ex-special forces, and unlike the other guys who said they were SAS, Banner actually was. Mattie had finally got the money together to get over to Africa, just as the bloody conflict had found a resolution. The civil war had left bodies everywhere. They were literally washing up on the shore, in the way that messages in bottles were supposed to but didn't. Over the six years of conflict, close to 200,000 people had been killed - and not one of the fuckers was down to Mattie. It was like going to a brothel and not getting laid.

It had cost Mattie two grand to get to the war zone, and

what he'd found was really disappointing. The men were nothing like the mercenaries he had seen in the movies. Most of them were just scum, plain and simple. They were thick, too. They even moaned about their time there. It used to drive Mattie mad. They had killed and sometimes even tortured. He should be the one moaning. He wasn't even getting paid, which would have been fine with him as long as he got to do a little killing.

The few who were good tended to stick together. They were all ex-forces and were paid a lot more than the others - and rightly so. Mattie wanted to live in a world where effort and skill were rewarded. He so much wanted to learn those skills. He had explained this to Banner, and it had paid off. A few of the top boys had been recruited to a new gig, and they asked him to come along. Mattie so much wanted to laugh in the face of the rest of the losers, for he was going to be part of a crack unit on UK shores.

When Banner had knighted him, Mattie knew the investment was worthwhile. His mother had always told him that he could be anything he wanted, and now that she was dead, he could be. The money from the will had helped him get to Africa, and while that hadn't worked out, it had helped him make connections. The rest of the money was what got him on the team. Mattie knew that this would probably be the best investment he would ever make. Once he had the skills down, he could go freelance.

Mattie Thompson: Assassin. It certainly had a nice ring to

it. And okay, so he wouldn't be paid - again. Mattie's mother had always said you had to speculate to accumulate, but she had died of cancer, so what did she know about anything? Mattie felt a wetness around his eyes. It sometimes happened. He wiped it away before the Cabbage Muncher could see.

. . .

Spencer was enjoying the best wank of his life when the phone rang. He hadn't phoned the agency in the end, fearing that in doing so he would simply be chasing the dragon. It was never going to be as good. That wasn't to say that he wouldn't be using the number the Emissary had given him again; he almost certainly would. For the first time in his life, Spencer was able to sample the buffet - there was no need to become fixated on any one vol-au-vent.

Spencer didn't know what had gotten into him in the last few days. He'd had an adequate enough sex drive in his twenties, even though there was rarely anyone on whom it could be used. Yet as he moved into his thirties and through to his forties, he found that whilst he was still interested in the idea of sex, the parts of his lower anatomy required less attentiveness. In truth, he had become less interested in life in general, and sex was just a part of that. He had put on a modicum of weight over this time, and whilst he didn't want to admit it was down to the malaise he felt, in his heart he knew it was true.

The Trent murder had changed all that. It had been a rebirth. Spencer had felt alive from the moment Trent's heart had stopped beating. At first it was nervous energy, but the night with Maria had refocused that energy, and his desire had flowered like a tulip in spring. Now he was erect more than he wasn't. It was almost becoming problematic.

The phone kept ringing, but Spencer was close and in no mood to delay the inevitable. He sped the up-and-down movement of his hand and pushed on to the end - an end that took him by surprise by its speed and ferocity. He didn't even have a chance to get the tissue on it.

Spencer picked up the phone with a sticky hand.

"Yes?" he said, his annoyance that the moment had been ruined clearly evident in his voice.

Spencer listened. What he heard made his penis shrink at a faster speed than was natural.

FOUR

Spencer met Banner within half an hour of receiving the phone call. He had walked up twelve flights of stairs to get to the roof, and when he reached his destination, he was out of breath and sweating profusely.

Banner greeted him with no more than a nod and handed Spencer a pair of binoculars. Spencer took a few deep breaths and waited for his heart rate to drop. Putting the glasses to his eyes, he looked to the building site below. It was quiet, free of people but for one man standing under the window of Colin Trent's flat. Spencer watched as the man paced forward, taking position, looking up towards where the neighbour's camera was and then looking at the ground under his feet.

"Who is he?" asked Spencer.

"He and a woman visited Trent's wife yesterday. They were there for twenty minutes. When they left, they went to the police station."

"Do we know what happened at the station?"

"They got squat. They were shown the videos and told there was nothing awry and to leave it."

"Do we have names?"

"David Mason and Alison Aimes. They run an internet magazine, readership practically none. We didn't think there was anything to worry about."

Spencer watched the trespasser walk up to the skip. The man picked up a nearby wooden pallet and threw it down next to a large container.

"Still think there's nothing to worry about? How did he get into the site?"

"The same way we did, I presume. There's something else. We got word from the station. He phoned, wanted to see the video again."

The man below picked up another pallet and laid it on top of the first to create a step. He stepped up onto the mini tower and looked down into the skip. Spencer watched as the man reached down and pulled out an object.

"You were told to remove everything from the site," said Spencer angrily. He lowered the binoculars and fixed Banner with a glare.

"It's a building site; it's hardly out of place. It was less risky than moving it."

Spencer's heart was pounding again, but it wasn't the exertion of climbing the stairs now. It had been the perfect crime. It had been over. But below him, this one little man had the potential to be the thread that unravelled all of his planning.

"What do you want to do?" asked Banner.

But Spencer was silent in thought.

. . .

Eleven o'clock came and went, and still there was no sign of David. Alison needed to inform Dante that there was an additional level of hell that he hadn't identified. Below the misers pushing heavy weights and the heretics and their burning tombs lay a circle of hell reserved for lone introverts at new-media conferences. It didn't help that she was paying money she didn't have for a raised table and a tiny 3 ft by 3 ft stall. Her audio/visual presentation wasn't pulling in the crowds, either; although that may have had something to do with the fact that they had run out of money and were limited to a handful of printed back-issue covers tacked onto partition walls.

On the bright side, Alison hadn't actually had to speak to anyone. She realised that this was somewhat of a qualified bright side, as the reason they had forked out the money was to make useful connections, yet as the magazine was finished, there didn't seem to be much to discuss.

Realising quickly that there wouldn't be an interested queue forming at her desk, she had deserted her post and taken a walk. Her perambulations had done nothing but make her feel old. The vast hangar of The Excel Centre was filled with stalls and businesses, every one of which seemed to be headed by people who were little more than foetuses with Justin Bieber haircuts. The video casters were the worst. Perky and youthful, they appeared to have God-like status. Even though they were completely unknown to Alison, they were getting all the attention here. The children had bloody groupies! Alison wasn't exactly sure when pointing a camera at yourself and talking about your hair stopped being pure narcissism and became an act deserving of displays of adulation on par with the Beatles arriving at JFK, but it had clearly happened.

Alison couldn't identify the moment she had stopped being young. Her youth was something that had passed her by while she wasn't looking. She was only thirty-six, and in truth she didn't feel any different than when she was twenty. It was clear looking around this room, though, that the true youth were a generation below her, and all seemed to be better looking and more successful than she had ever been.

Alison looked at her mobile again. There was still no message from David. He had sent a text at eight saying that he was going to look at something. What that "something" involved was not spelt out, but it wasn't unusual for David's messages to be of the vague variety. Alison sent another text. This would be her fourth. It wasn't like him. He knew that she wouldn't want to do this on her own. He was the extrovert in the relationship. David would have taken their tiny badly organised stall and made it a place people wanted to visit just by force of personality. He had always loved the limelight.

It had been fifteen years since she had gone to that Islington pub. She had climbed the steps to the tiny theatre and had been one of nineteen people in the audience. David had asked her to attend, and thinking back on that night, she remembered just how nervous she had been. They had been friends for only a couple of months by that point, and Alison enjoyed his company and really didn't want to ruin it by not being able to hide her embarrassment.

She needn't have worried. When David came on stage, it was like gazing upon someone else. It wasn't the clothes or the makeup, it was just him, the way he carried himself, the way he spoke. She watched her friend transform, and in doing so she became immersed in the story. She had cried that night in a way that she hadn't cried at the theatre before or since. Maybe it was the play - more likely it was pride in a friend who made those tears happen, along with a feeling that a bright future lay ahead of both of them.

Alison looked at the empty chair next to her. Where was he? She tried phoning again, but the call went straight to voicemail. In the pit of her stomach, Alison felt fear.

. . .

By four, Alison had decided to pack up and go home. There was still no word from David. She had spoken to only eight people all day, and it was clear that those attendees who remained were circulating only to pick up any freebies on offer. But Alison had no freebies.

If truth be told, Alison had only signed up for the conference because she wanted to show a commitment to the decision she had made. She thought that by now they would have a handful of employees and a good reputation. So successful would the magazine be that there would be a veritable queue of people wanting to talk to them about their writing and the mysteries they had investigated. Yet as the weeks of insufficient subscriptions had led to months of insubstantial profits, it had become clear that this event was not going to the statement of victory of which she had dreamed.

Alison started to remove the covers from the wall. Maybe, years from now, she would look back on these pages with pride, but at that moment she felt little more than sadness.

The blue tack stuck to the felt, and it was when Alison was trying to scratch it off with her nail that she heard a cough behind her. She turned to see a bearded man smiling at her through thick spectacles.

"Hi," said Alison, smiling.

"I always liked your magazine. I subscribed."

Of the now nine people that she had spoken to, he was the first who had shown any knowledge of what she did.

"Unfortunately, you were one of the few, it seems. But thank you. It's appreciated."

"You were maybe too early or too late."

"Or maybe people didn't want a magazine investigating

unanswered questions," said Alison.

"People don't know what they want. Or what's good for them. If we don't ask questions, then we are at the will of the people who seek to control us."

It was at that moment that Alison knew that he was one of them. He was a conspiracy theorist. The truth was that these were the people that had kept the magazine going for as long as it had. The original brief was to stay away from anything that reeked of the tinfoil-hat brigade, but those editions had proved less popular then the more nutbar fare. In the end, they had moved over to full-on "out there" reporting. They had even questioned the evidence of the moon landings - at which point Alison knew that she had properly sold out.

The magazine had never gone as far as to say the moon landings had been faked - in fact, if anything they had debunked most of the evidence on show. But the very fact that they were even entertaining the conversation meant that they had lost the game. Now Alison and David were looked at by those conspiracy theorists as one of their own.

The bearded man reached into his pocket and pulled out a business card. It just had the name Stephen Manson on the front and an email address. He dropped the card on the table in front of Alison.

"You would be Stephen Manson?" said Alison, holding out her hand.

"That is the name I go by," said Manson, shaking her hand and somewhat eluding the question.

"What do you do, Mr Manson?"

"I fight the fight. And provide equipment to those that do likewise. People like you."

Alison considered her response. If there was a possibility of publishing another edition, she would probably have said nothing. She certainly couldn't afford to annoy one of her few subscribers. But the magazine wasn't a going concern.

"I think you may have mistaken my position on a number of items. You see, I don't believe in conspiracies, Mr Manson. They rely too much on the need for government secrecy and efficiency. I used to work in government - and both efficiency and secrecy are in very short supply."

FIVE

The problem with running a huge conspiracy was that you always had to be on top of your game. There had been a glitch, and Spencer had dealt with it. Decisive action had been taken, and any chance of the secret unravelling had been nullified. That was the difference that made the difference. Leadership really was his forte.

It was Spencer's day off, and being free of MI5, the last place he really wanted to be was stuck on surveillance. But good management was about leading by example, and now that Banner was out of the picture for a few days, he would have to lay down his authority. He had gone to the hotel and given the troops their orders, then signed on for surveillance of Sally Constance, the biker's girlfriend. Spencer had allocated himself to this task mostly because he didn't fancy anything that involved walking. Now, in hindsight, he realised this was a bad decision. He had been excited to speak privately to Cosmin Alexe, who had, in his time, been a legend in the Romanian Securitate. The truth was however that, whilst Mr Alexe may have been great company in the eighties, in later years he had turned into the world's most boring man.

The van was one of three that had been purchased by the Emissary, based on Spencer's list. How the Emissary had got hold of three brand-new surveillance vans was a mystery to Spencer, but in truth, no matter the quality of the van, the act still involved being in a confined space while looking at video of nothing very much happening. That was always going to be challenging, but when the living legend you are with has nothing to talk about but bird-watching, time really does drag.

Spencer had phoned the Emissary when the complication had arisen. The Emissary had reminded him that the Russian was a man of limited patience, but Spencer had convinced him that everything was under control, and the Emissary had done what was asked of him. The Russian had obviously run into trouble in the past and was well known for his ruthless reputation. Although, not wanting to ruin his guise as a legitimate, if elusive, businessman, he was never going to actually get his hands dirty.

Few knew what the Russian looked like. Spencer had met him, but by that point he had crossed the line so far that there was no going back. The Russian owned him from the moment Spencer had passed over the information. He often thought about that decision. In times of weakness, he would question the choice he made. But weakness was exactly what it was. He knew he had no reason to feel guilty. His information had led to the death of a man, but so what? It wasn't like the man in question was ever going to make Pope. Maybe the man who met that grisly end wasn't a monster, but he was damn close. Spencer may have blood on his hands, but that was a trickle compared to the amount that covered the "victims."

Spencer had been forced to make the hard decision over and over again in the name of the Crown. Actions had been sanctioned, and people had been sacrificed along the way. This was the way of the world. Spencer knew that sometimes there was a need to get dirty. The people in their beds loved to think how good and moral they were. Well, that morality was founded on the backs of people like him.

As Spencer watched the monitor, he felt his eyes growing heavy. Maybe it was the heat, or the lack of anything happening, but most probably it was the talk of Cosmin Alexe once seeing a condor. But then on the screen the door to the biker's house opened, and a woman walked out. She was small, blonde, and about as different to the type Spencer usually went for as it would be possible to find. She was undoubtedly very attractive, but that really couldn't explain the way she made him feel.

He watched as the woman locked the door and walked out of the house. She walked to a red Mini Cooper, opened the door, and climbed inside.

"Follow her!" said Spencer with a level of excitement that

surprised even him.

As the van moved away, Spencer repositioned himself to accommodate his erection. He worried that his comrade might notice the bulge, but the man seemed way too interested in discussing the threat to birds of prey to notice anything penile.

. . .

It was seven in the morning when Alison rang the doorbell to David's flat and received no response. She had phoned and texted numerous times, but still there was no sign of him. Alison and David had kept copies of each other's keys for years, and it was with that spare key that Alison opened the front door. She was met by a meowing tabby called Boots, named after a character from a Christmas Panto that David had played in four years earlier. Alison bent down to stroke the cat, and the animal reciprocated the attention by rubbing its body against her leg. When she had visited in the past, Boots had not been anywhere near that friendly, which led Alison to believe that the cat was either starved of company or just starved. Both possibilities were worrisome. It meant that David hadn't been home.

Alison called David's name as she walked into the flat. There was no response. She moved through to the living room and then on to the kitchen. The sight of two empty cat bowls added further to her concern.

Alison opened a can of cat food, dished it into the bowl, and placed it on the floor for Boots, who ate rapidly. She moved into the living room and turned her attention to the phone. Putting the handset to her ear, she heard an intermittent ringtone which showed that there were messages. Alison dialled 1571 and listened. There were four messages; three from her and one from David's agent asking where the hell he was.

. . .

Spencer was thinking about Sally Constance. He had spent four hours yesterday following the woman, and the thought still excited him so much that he'd had to visit the Thames House toilets for relief. As he moved his hand up and down his erection, he pictured her face.

He knew that she was thirty-two, an age far older then Spencer usually went for. But then, when you're paying you're always going to go young. At thirty-two, she was still over a decade his junior.

As Spencer continued to move his hand up and down, he imagined her lying on his bed, opening her legs, willing him to come forward and take her. But as Spencer held the image in his mind, he could feel himself becoming distracted by the man who had brushed away the honour of which Spencer was now fantasising. That damn biker. He had been a pain from day one, but now he was intruding on Spencer's wanking time, and that simply wasn't right.

Spencer had expected to find the biker by now, but still he was a fugitive. How bloody difficult was it to find and kill a man? Those he had hired were supposed to be the best in the business. The man they were chasing had no training. It should have been the equivalent of shooting fish in a barrel. They knew he was in the country; they had the best information the British Secret Service could provide at their fingertips, and still there was no sign of him. The man was a ghost.

They had known who he was early enough. The Egyptians had got that right at least. He had left his bike in the desert. It was clear that after they lost him they had sat around expecting him to die, but when it became obvious that this had not happened they had at least passed his passport details over.

He'd thought that their quarry would head straight home, but the evidence was that Ms Constance had not had contact with the biker. Spencer thought that she would be the key. Surely no man could stay away from a woman that fine? He would become an expert in the life of the woman. What she saw in some lank-haired biker was beyond Spencer.

He had ordered copies of Ms Constance's phone records. The bugs in her house were recording, and the pages of her diary had been photocopied. They had made the excursion into her flat over a week ago, but so far it had led to nothing. Spencer could be patient - he just hoped that the Russian could as well. He had been a professional voyeur in the lives of hundreds in his career, all without worry, but for some reason Spencer found this time different - mostly because he found her different.

It was no use. His erection had died. He needed to find the biker soon. He was already missing his newfound sex drive.

Spencer reached into his pocket and pulled out a mobile. The phone had been taken from the construction-site snooper when he was snatched. Spencer knew he would destroy the phone before the day was out, but first he wanted to see who was missing him. The phone bleeped, and the text icon showed there were ten new texts. Nine of those texts were from the woman named Alison, and as he flicked through, he saw each successive text displaying increasing concern. Spencer considered his options. He looked through the snooper's texts, and once he felt able to mimic the man's text voice, he typed:

'Am fine. Just needed time to think. D x'

And he pressed send.

The remaining text was from an acting agent. Spencer suddenly felt better about life. He was about to reduce the competition for at least one new RADA graduate.

Spencer switched off the phone. He pulled open the back, removed the sim, and flushed it down the toilet with his unused wank paper.

. . .

Mattie was bored. Bored and fed up. Bored, fed up, and pissed off. This was rubbish. He was supposed to be doing some killing, and yet so far he hadn't even punched anyone.

He had been punched. And kicked. Those bloody commies. They were on his back every fucking second. That twat of a boss was no help. He was as useful as a chocolate teapot, as his mother used to say. She never used to say it often, though, because she didn't like speaking badly of people. Even people who really deserved to be spoken badly of - like the bastard she had married.

Mattie was waiting again. So far the fat suit-wearing twat had achieved precisely nothing. There was talk of a murder that had happened, but the information was kept on a need-to-know basis. That was what they had told him, although it did seem to Mattie that he was the only sod who didn't need to know. That pissed him off even more. For fuck's sake, he wasn't the tea boy, so why did everyone keep treating him like he was some kind of fucking idiot?

And what had they achieved in the last week? Nothing, that's what. Suddenly Mattie's idea of going in there and slicing information out of people didn't seem so bad, did it? They certainly would have been no worse off - and more importantly for Mattie, they would have gotten some nice violence in. That was what this whole bloody shebang was missing - a little bit of graphic eighteen-certificated torture porn.

Mattie could have done it as well. Sod the commie dicks and their stupid methods. They hadn't seen Hostel eight times like he had. Critics and intellectuals always said Casablanca was the best film ever, but Mattie thought that was bollocks.

Hostel was a million times better, and any idiot could see it. First of all, it was in colour. Casablanca was black and white, and thus shit. More importantly, Casablanca didn't have any brilliant torture. Play it Sam? Fuck that! Remove Sam's eyeballs with a scalpel. See if he can play the fucking piano then.

Mattie's mind was wandering. He was thinking about films when he should be working. Well, if this counted as working, which it didn't, then he had failed, but it wasn't so it didn't. Something like that. Mattie's mind was all over the place - but that's what happens when you stare at a computer monitor for seven hours.

The computers had been set up in the basement, and the walls around Mattie were bare brick and crumbling. Mattie guessed it had probably been the laundry room when the place was a hotel because the room seemed to have a smell of cleanliness that worked against the grubby visuals.

That had been the case until the tech guy showed up, at which point the aroma of cleanliness was replaced by the distinct fragrance of skunk cannabis. The tech had been scruffy with long greasy hair. He had sat in front of the computer next to Mattie for less than twenty minutes, but the smell remained long after the man had left. Mattie had never used drugs, and he didn't trust anyone that did. The lack of trust seemed mutual, however, as the small amount of conversation showed that the tech guy knew far more than Mattie. It also was clear that he had no intention of sharing that knowledge.

Mattie looked at the YouTube clip again. It was bloody busy

work. Put the tea boy away where he can't get into bother while everyone goes off to have adventures and kill people. Let him play on the computer. Let him watch videos of idiots who think aliens exist. It didn't even look real. It looked like rubber tubing. Those were not real intestines. Mattie knew what those looked like. And again, Hostel came into the picture. That's what a good film did for you. It changed the way you saw the world for the better.

Maybe the door wasn't locked, but it had been made clear to him that he shouldn't leave. The boss said it was important work. Was it shit!

He had been given the task of looking through a bunch of online magazines called Enigma. Mattie thought it was a rubbish title. There were twenty videos, all about five minutes long, but they were nothing more than trailers for the magazines rather than being something good - like TV. At first Mattie thought it wouldn't be too bad. The magazine looked like it was going to investigate really interesting stuff. Mattie got excited when he saw that they were looking into the moon landings but was very confused when the magazine said there was no evidence of a hoax. Mattie knew it was a hoax; he had seen a film about it on YouTube.

With the magazines read, Mattie had gone through the posted comments, as ordered, and logged details. He followed any links that had been posted and wrote down details of where the link led. That was the reason he was now looking at a video showing an alleged alien autopsy. Enigma magazine may have been sleep inducing, but it was clear that the people that read it had more exotic tastes. They were full-out nuts.

Mattie had paid lots of money for adventure, and he was wasting time doing office work. He had tried to piece together the great plan from snippets of overheard conversation. It was clear that the left hand didn't know that the right hand was wanking. What's more, everyone had got a lot more secretive with him since it was made fairly obvious that the boss didn't think he could be trusted. How was he supposed to make sense of these bloody conspiracy videos if he didn't know any of the fucking context?

Mattie felt lost. He had found such certainty after his mother had died. He was a bad man. Evil. How could he have come from the loins of that bastard and not be? There was an inevitability to Mattie's existence. From birth, he was destined to be this…monster. But if that was the hand he had been dealt, he was going to use it to be the best he could be. Life had given him lemons, and Mattie was going to make Sprite.

Mattie's bastard father had the monster within him, of that there was no doubt, but he had wasted it on beating up his wife and a child too small to defend himself. When he got tired of that and tried to move up in the world, he had been found wanting and ended up inside for a ten stretch. He had wasted his talents. Mattie was going to do more. And yet here he was watching shitty internet videos.

Mattie clicked another link and found himself looking at a YouTube video where a specky twat was talking about the hidden messages in the film The Shining. Maybe his movie knowledge would come in useful after all.

SIX

Alison really wasn't used to getting up this early. A handful of masochists had been waiting outside the gym before it had even opened. They had all piled in at six a.m., and now Alison was alone. Although the day showed all the signs of being pleasant, at this hour it was chilly, and Alison shivered as she was caught by a cool breeze.

She had phoned the police station last night and was told the gym was where she could find Inspector Grant. Knowing Grant's problems at the station, she felt guilty for door stepping him. But with her best friend missing, she felt it only right to let good manners take a back seat.

Alison had received a text yesterday, allegedly from David, but while the syntax may have been similar to his usual messages, it didn't make sense in context. For an often gregarious man, David had always been direct in his electronic communication. The few times he would ever use more than the bare minimum of words was when he needed to apologise - and even then, he usually would do this in person, or at least by phone. He would have known how awkward she would have found the conference and been effusive in his apology, but instead there was a text of only a few words. It wasn't just out of character - it clearly wasn't David.

She looked up to see a figure running towards her. She had met Grant only two days ago, but in this new context it took her a moment to realise it was him. The suit had been replaced by jogging bottoms and a sweaty red T-shirt. When she'd seen him before he hadn't looked like a man who was comfortable in a suit, but Alison didn't think he looked particularly comfortable in leisure wear, either. She wondered whether there existed a fashion that suited the man.

Grant saw Alison and slowed. He stopped in front of her, an angry expression on his face, quickly forced away as he realised he was hideously out of breath.

"You're waiting for me?"

Alison nodded.

"How did you know I would be here?" asked Grant, looking confused.

"The people at the station really hate you. You must have really pissed them off."

"Well, it's been great," said Grant, pushing his way past

Alison, clearly in no mood to chat.

"David is missing." blurted Alison.

Grant stopped, turned to look at her.

"I'm not Missing Persons."

"It may be linked to the Trent murder."

Grant remained silent for a moment.

"He contacted me two days ago," said Grant. "He asked me for a copy of the video."

"What did you tell him?"

"I told him I wasn't running a bloody video rental service and to bugger off."

"He's been missing for two days. Please. Can we talk?"

Grant looked at Alison with a look of exasperation. "I can meet you at lunchtime. There is a café around the corner. Royals. I will meet you there at one. And you're buying."

. . .

Grant shovelled a piece of egg-covered sausage into his mouth.

The café was busy, and practically every table was taken by lunching office workers. Lunch had cost Alison ten pounds, which she really couldn't afford, but in providing the ability to speak to somebody about her friend's disappearance, albeit between mouthfuls of fried food, the investment had been a good one.

"What evidence do you have that his disappearance is related to the Trent murder?" asked Grant.

"None. But it was the only thing we were working on. He sent a text saying he was going to look at something."

Grant shrugged. "Doesn't mean it had anything to do with Trent. Maybe he had a personal issue?"

Alison shook her head. "He would have talked it over with me."

"Maybe he didn't want to?"

"David and I have been best friends for over a decade. We tell each other everything. And even if we didn't, there is no way he would just leave and not say anything. It's not in character."

"People do things that are out of character all the time. They go off the radar and then turn up again a few days later. You said you received a text from him?"

"But it wasn't him. He wouldn't have just sent a one-line text. He would have called me. I went to his house. He hadn't fed his cat. He wouldn't have done that."

"If you are worried, speak to Missing Persons. I can give you a number."

"We look into an alleged murder of a prominent journalist, I get a message from David saying he is looking into something, and at the same time, you get a phone call from him requesting the DVD. He then disappears without trace."

"Except you got a text where he says he's fine."

"Come on. Do you honestly think this isn't at least suspicious?"

Grant was silent for a moment. Alison thought that he may

be looking to continue eating, but instead he reached into his pocket and pulled out an A5 envelope. He placed it down in front of Alison, who picked it up. She looked inside to find a stick drive.

"I put the DVD onto a stick drive. I can't look into it. I'm not Missing Persons. If you want to go through it, fine, but you didn't get a copy from me. Understood?"

"Thank you," said Alison.

"Don't thank me yet. I have gone through every frame. If there's something there, I couldn't find it."

. . .

Sitting in his home, a flat which was now unquestionably too small for a man of his status, it dawned on Spencer that his priorities truly were all over the place. The Emissary had again informed him that the Russian was getting impatient. A few days ago, the world had seemed such a promising place. He had pulled off an impossible murder. The Russian should be thanking him still, but now it seemed the tide had turned. What did the man expect?

The biker was being smart, that was for sure, but Spencer was smarter. The biker hadn't withdrawn any money from his bank, but how long could he resist doing so? All of his recognised friends had been checked out, and bugs had been placed where necessary. Spencer even had operatives walking the streets looking for beggars. Everyone believed they would be able to disappear if it came down to it, but Spencer knew that people always left traces. He just needed to wait for the biker to make a mistake. That was the way the game worked. It was just a shame for Spencer that the Russian didn't seem to think the same way.

The additional request Spencer had made of the Russian had not helped, but what did he expect Spencer to do? The Emissary had shown surprise that he had not just shot the snooper on the spot. That might well work in other places, but in England public assassinations tended to result in lots of questions. The solution Spencer had come up with might be resource heavy, including reducing the manpower of his team for a short while, but it had been the best option in terms of controlling the narrative. That was why Spencer had been hired, to see the bigger picture. He wasn't just a savage; he was a Machiavellian game player.

The snooper would be dealt with, but first Spencer wanted to see how the snooper's female friend would react. He had sources at the station waiting for a missing person's report to come in, but so far there was nothing. When the woman did eventually go to the police, there were people in place who could render the investigation unworthy of continuation. But if the woman took another route, Spencer wanted to have a bargaining chip in hand. It was a safety plan that was never going to be needed, but Spencer always believed in planning for the best and preparing for the worst.

It was fine. Spencer was just over worrying. Maybe he

needed to phone the agency - that would relax him. Yet try as he might to concentrate on Eastern European prostitutes, Spencer couldn't get one face out of his head. It was a face that he had first seen on a video monitor less than twenty-four hours earlier.

Spencer picked up his iPod. He had requested the recordings from Ms Constance's flat be downloaded, and he had been listening to them whenever he had a spare moment. Now the evening was his, and he wanted to share it with her. He was tired. The two-jobs situation would have to be taken care of - yet the thought of hearing her talk privately to him gave him energy.

Spencer walked to his stereo. He pressed a button, and the room was filled with the sound of Strauss. Spencer let the music envelop him. And as he moved his body to the waltz, he placed his earbuds in his ears and heard her voice and the music together. He imagined she was there with him, in his arms, and they were dancing cheek to cheek.

Maybe he needed to worry. Maybe his deal with the Russian had not been a good idea. But tonight, none of that would matter, because he had her.

. . .

Alison felt her eyes closing but fought to stay awake. She had been watching the video for the past five hours, and as far as she could tell, there really was nothing to see. Alison moved from her reclining position on the sofa and sat upright. She needed to keep watching. If David had asked for these videos, it was because he'd expected to see something. But even upright, Alison's tiredness won out, and by the time the clock rolled over to 3am, she was asleep.

SEVEN

Alison exited the lift into a corridor largely identical to the one she had found a few days earlier, when she had visited Isabella Trent. Only the pictures on the wall were different, although not so much that they dispelled a vague feeling of déjà vu. She knew that the video was taken directly opposite Trent's flat and so must have been taken from one of the properties towards the end of the corridor. Alison had been told that the building was mostly deserted, so in the worst-case scenario, she would knock on every door until someone opened up. In the end that wasn't necessary, as when she rang the bell of the flat at the far end of the corridor, the door was opened by a smartly suited avuncular man in his sixties.

"Mr Wearing?" asked Alison.

The man smiled broadly. "Come in, my dear," said Wearing.

Alison walked into the flat. The cheery welcome was certainly not what she had been led to expect from the description offered at the police station.

The flat was identical in layout to Colin Trent's but reversed - as if viewed in a mirror. But where Trent's flat had been sparsely decorated, this flat was covered from floor to ceiling in books.

Wearing pointed her towards a comfortable-looking high-backed chair. He pulled out a dining chair from a nearby table and sat directly opposite her. Either he was preparing for an in-depth chat, or she was going to be interrogated.

"So what can I do for you?" asked Wearing.

As he said this, there was a loud hollow bang from the building site outside, causing him to noticeably stiffen. He caught himself and smiled again broadly towards Alison.

"It's about your video," said Alison.

"Sorry?" said Wearing, confusion now evident on his face.

"Your video of the construction site."

"So you are not my 11am appointment?" He asked, looking confused.

"No. I just wanted to ask you a few questions."

"Wait!" said Wearing. "Do you work for those fuckers?" He stood up angrily.

"No. I—"

Alison was interrupted by a series of loud bangs. She could feel the vibration even through the soft padding of the chair.

Wearing walked quickly to the window. He threw it open and stuck his head through. "Shut up, you bastards!" he screamed at the top of his voice.

And then Wearing turned back towards Alison, the anger now evident on his face. "You work for them, don't you? They have sent you here to trick me."

"Mr Wearing, I don't work for anyone. I just wanted to ask you about your video. I think it may help in my friend's disappearance."

"What are you talking about?"

"Please, Mr Wearing, I just wanted to ask you about your video and Colin Trent."

"Colin Trent?"

Yes," replied Alison. "I think my friend has been taken because he found out how he was murdered."

Wearing reverted to the smiling man as quickly as he had turned to rage.

"You will forgive me, my dear. The noise outside does render me somewhat irrational. I am afraid I can't talk for long. I have an eleven o'clock meeting, you see."

"What do you do, Mr Wearing?"

"I'm a psychoanalyst," said Wearing.

As he said it, the banging resumed, and Wearing's face flickered to anger, and then flickered again back to smiling, like a faulty connection on a light of pure rage. If this man was the psychoanalyst, how crazy were his patients?

"They are supposed to work set hours. But they don't. The noise is pretty much twenty-four-seven," continued Wearing.

"What hours are they supposed to work?"

"Nine to four, Monday to Friday only," replied Wearing.

Something in the statement bothered Alison, but it took her a moment to work out what it was.

"Colin Trent died on a Saturday. The video shows building work going on, but you said they were only supposed to work weekdays?" said Alison.

"Why do you think I was taping them?" said Wearing. "They don't stick to the rules."

"Did they work weekends often?"

He shook his head. "Just long hours, usually."

"Did they ever work Saturdays before?"

Wearing thought about the question for a while and then answered, "No."

. . .

Mattie walked towards the third hostel of the day. Finally, he had been given something worthwhile to do. There was no murdering involved yet, but at least he was away from the commies, and the way things had developed back at the hotel that was a good thing.

His time in the hotel had not been fun, if he was honest - and Mattie was always honest. The commies had started calling him Moppi. At first Mattie thought this was a good thing - all cool kids have a nickname, after all. It was Andreas the German who started it. He had walked up to Mattie and told him they had decided on the new nickname. And then they'd all pissed themselves laughing and barking. Mattie had gone to his room after that. It was like bloody school over again.

The more things change, the more they stay the same, thought Mattie.

Mattie had been briefed on his new role by the tosspot when he had visited for one of his infrequent visits to the hotel. He had another new suit, and it looked expensive. It was clear that this man was making big bucks. It pissed Mattie off.

He had been given the job of visiting hostels to see if they had seen the biker. It was a job that, up until now, had been reserved for the Brits, as it was easier for them to pretend that they were the biker's family. But Banner and most of the other Brits had been noticeable by their absence over the past couple of days. Mattie wondered where they were. Now all the good guys had gone and just the commies remained. What's worse, it meant that the alpha, Cabbage Muncher, was now king. Mattie should have gone with the Brits, wherever they were. It was not that Mattie hated foreigners. It was just that he hated these foreigners.

He walked through the door and into the hostel. Only a few minutes from Camden, it was hidden away from the main market street, thus saving free-spending tourists the unappetising sight of the homeless. Inside the hostel was clean and basic, with a handful of people hanging around that could best be described as sketchy. It was, in short, not very different to the lobby of a Travelodge.

There were people queued at the front desk, so Mattie turned his attention to the noticeboard attached to the wall. In between the adverts for jobs and lists of lost property were a handful of missing-person notices. Pictures of those being searched for had been pinned to the wall, accompanied by short notes from the family about how much the people were missed. The pictures made Mattie sad. Maybe it was the pictures, maybe it was the realisation that his father and brother would never have put up notices like this for him or maybe it was that there was now nobody who cared if he was missing or not. Mattie felt alone.

Mattie brushed away the bleak thoughts from his mind. He had a job to do. He had to find the biker and kill him. Or kill someone at least. If he wasn't allowed to kill soon, Mattie was going to explode - literally.

. . .

Alison banged on the gate for the third time. In front of her, a sign declared hard hats and boots were to be worn. She had neither, but that was proving moot, as no one seemed overly keen on creating an opening in the fence.

Finally the gate was dragged open, and a helmeted construction worker stared back at her.

"Yes?"

"I'd like to see the boss," said Alison.

"You got an appointment?" asked the builder gruffly.

Alison shook her head. "No."

"Can't come in, then," said the construction worker unapologetically.

"He will want to speak with me." Alison tried to project confidence but felt certain that it wasn't working. She needed answers to questions, but knew she was only going to get them at the speed she needed with a face-to-face conversation.

"Why?" asked the builder.

An idea came to her. She put her hand on her stomach. Looked at the builder, and with fake tears welling, she said, "Because he's the father."

David had spent several hours teaching Alison core acting skills. The importance of believing in the lie. The need to become the character. She had never reached anywhere near his ability, but when called for, the skill set could be useful.

The builder weighed up his options. "Better come in, then."

David would have been proud.

Alison walked through the gate and was led to a large hut that obviously passed for a site office. The builder opened the door and waved her in.

"You can find him in there," he said as he closed the door behind her.

At the front of the office was a desk with a computer, phone, and assorted papers. Alison could see a larger room behind the partition wall, where a man and woman were talking. She guessed that this was the PAs area and that the room beyond was the lair of the manager. As there was no one at the front desk, Alison surmised that female voice was probably the PA, with the male voice belonging to the man she needed to see.

She walked forward, through the door in the partition wall and into the larger office. The man and woman were seated at an oversized desk. It was out of place in this hut and struck Alison as the desk of someone who needed people to know he was the boss—either that or this man truly had a failed understanding of spatial reasoning.

"Hello," said Alison, smiling.

The man and woman looked over to her.

The man behind the large desk was balding. His suit glistened against the sunlight coming through the small window. His body language shouted "boss", but it was the added detail of the suit and desk combined that shouted "wanker." Across from him, the woman had a notebook in front of her. Alison guessed that this must be his PA, and everything she had seen so far suggested that it was probably the job from hell.

"Can I help you?" said the boss, checking Alison out as he did so.

"I just wanted to ask you a couple of questions."

The boss turned towards the PA. "Take a break please, Cindy. Leave us to talk."

The PA pulled away from the desk and headed for the door. Alison wondered if her short skirt was expected.

With Cindy gone, Alison held out her hand. "Alison."

The boss stared at her coldly. "Have you been sent by my wife?"

Alison paused. "No."

The boss smiled. He reached out and shook Alison's hand warmly.

"Jack," he said. "Please, take a seat." He pointed to the seat vacated by the PA. Alison sat. "Now then, what can I do for you?" said Jack slimily.

"I just have one question, really: Do your workers work on Saturday?"

"Probably - although not for me." Jack smiled.

"What, never?"

"Have you been listening to that old sod opposite?"

Alison nodded. "I have met Mr Wearing. He is a strange one."

"He's an arrogant, mad fool is what he is."

"He has video of your site operating on a Saturday."

"His video is set wrong. Old fool probably doesn't know what button to press."

"We have police experts who say that the video is accurate."

"What can I say? Your police experts are incorrect. It costs me double time if they come in Saturday - not to mention that it's against our contract. It would please Wearing no end if we did actually work the hours he claimed. It would add some credence to his unsubstantiated lies. The man is only happy when he's miserable."

"Would it help if I showed you the video?" said Alison.

He shrugged. "The video that is wrong? Sure, knock yourself out."

"Can I use your computer?"

He pushed his laptop towards her, and she reached into her bag and pulled out the stick drive. She slotted it in. The laptop whirred, and the video quadrants popped up. Alison pointed to the lower-right colour footage.

"That's Mr Wearing's camera. You see the date stamp? It's a Saturday."

Jack looked at the screen as the jumping colour pictures advanced every few seconds, making the few construction workers move like Aardman got lazy.

"Those are not my workers," said Jack. His face had hardened, the smarm had disappeared and had been replaced by genuine concern.

"Sorry?"

"I know my workers."

"You can tell from those pictures?"

"I'm around them all bloody day! Of course I can tell." He jumped up from his chair.

"Where are you going?"

"Wearing is not the only one with CCTV footage. There's a lot of expensive equipment here."

"You have video and you didn't notice this before?"

He shook his head. "There was no need. There was no sign of a break-in, and nothing is missing."

He moved to a cabinet attached to the wall, secured by a numerical lock. Jack covered up the keys as he pressed them, and the cabinet clicked. He pulled the handle, and the doors opened up to reveal a monitor. Below the monitor there were two computer towers, a keyboard, and a mouse. Jack moved the mouse, and the monitor flashed to life. He pulled up an index and clicked on the date of Trent's murder. The grainy black-and-white videos showed up on the screen, split into eight CCTV images.

More black-and-white images was not something Alison thought she would want to see, but unlike the video she had been watching, this at least offered to elucidate rather than confuse.

"This is top of the line," boasted Jack. "My brother put it in."

He looked pleased with himself. Moving the mouse, the eight images went into fast forward.

"What time does your tape show?" asked Jack.

"The segment you saw, 4.15 p.m. The tape ran forward. Alison felt the tension increase as it got closer to the matching time. She watched in horror as, one by one, each of the eight screens was replaced by static.

"That can't be," said Jack. "It's a ten-grand system."

"It looks like your ten-grand system has been compromised," said Alison. Her pleasure in seeing this man's bluster deflated was tempered heavily by the reality that the video could not help in finding David.

Jack ran the tape forward at 180x speed. Static filled the frame for about a minute, and then the eight pictures returned. He looked at the screen in shock.

"What the hell happened here?"

"Have you got any other CCTV images?"

He shook his head. "No, every camera comes through onto this computer here," he said, pointing to the right-hand stack.

"Then what's on the other computer?"

Alison could tell that Jack was flustered. He had been confused, and in that moment he'd let something slip. There was something about the computer that he didn't want her to know.

"It's just… stuff. Technical," he said, his smarmy articulation suddenly deserting him.

"Stuff?" asked Alison, fixing him with a questioning gaze.

"Sorry I couldn't help. I will speak with my brother and see if he can explain what went wrong," said Jack, momentarily breaking eye contact before catching himself and bringing his eyes back to her. He was lying.

But Alison had become fixated on the other computer. She looked closely and followed the lead through the cabinet and down the wall.

"What are you looking for?" asked Jack, the concern clear in his voice.

Alison just kept following the lead across the bottom of the front wall, through to the side wall before disappearing under the carpet at a point closest to the desk.

"I really have to insist you leave," said Jack.

Alison, like a bloodhound on a trail, walked in a straight line towards the desk—that large desk at which he had been so keen for her to sit. Maybe it was nothing. Maybe it was her being overly suspicious. Even so, she moved to the front of the desk and kneeled and looked underneath.

"This is getting silly, please leave," said Jack with a firmness that couldn't disguise his growing unease.

But when Alison looked under her desk, she saw what she suspected. Now she knew how much this man would have appreciated his PA's short skirts—because Alison was looking straight at a camera.

"You pervert!" Alison said, staring at him in disgust.

"It's not what it looks like."

"Then what is it? Because to me it certainly seems that you have a camera under your desk for no other purpose than upskirt shots."

"Okay. It is what it looks like. But… it's just a bit of fun."

Alison stood upright and faced him. She was trying to contain a fury that was about to boil over.

"Fun. You son of a bitch. I feel violated."

"It wasn't for you. Anyway, you have trousers on. There's not going to be anything to see."

"And that makes it all right? I noticed your PA didn't have trousers on when she was sitting here."

Jack paled visibly. "Please don't tell her."

"Why shouldn't I?"

"Because I love her." He was close to tears now, every ounce of confidence gone.

"So. Let's look at the other computer, shall we?"

83

"Please, no."

"If you don't want me to go straight out there and speak to your PA, I want to see what that camera recorded on that Saturday."

He shook his head. "It doesn't work that way. It's motion sensitive. It only records when there's something directly in front of the camera."

"Well, let's see if anything was, shall we?"

. . .

Jack eventually relented, but it took ten minutes for him to switch the left-hand computer to the monitor. It had required the input of three passwords to get this far, a procedure far more detailed than had been required for the CCTV images. This was a secret that had been closely guarded and one that hopefully stopped the burglars gaining access.

Jack pulled up the index. The list of dates included the Saturday Trent was murdered.

"There are three clips from that day."

"Click it," said Alison impatiently.

"First I want some guarantees."

"What?"

"I will show you this image. I will print out any image that identifies those that were trespassing, but only if you promise to not say anything to Cindy or the police."

"You expect me to just leave without that poor woman

knowing that you have been wanking over video of her crotch?"

"If you want to see what is on that screen, that's exactly what I expect. The question is how much you want to see this image?"

Alison fumed. She wanted to bring this man down, but for David's sake, she needed to see what was on the video.

"You have my word: I won't say anything to your PA."

"Or the police."

"Or the police," agreed Alison.

"Right then, let's see what we can see, shall we." A now smiling Jack clicked the mouse. Alison felt like punching the git.

On the screen, through the archway formed by the underside of the desk, a pair of trousered legs could be seen. Before Alison could make sense of the image, the legs disappeared as the man walked away.

"Damn!" exclaimed Alison.

But then the video clicked on again, and she saw a different pair of legs. But those legs also walked away, and the screen turned to black.

The screen came to life once more. But the three-quarter shot of a pair of legs wasn't going to be of much use. Alison realised that she was holding her breath. She exhaled, and as she did so, she watched the man bend to tie his shoelaces. Alison looked at the face of the man. The image was blurred, the camera being set for closer focus, but from what she could tell, the man somewhat surprisingly looked like a pensioner.

. . .

Jack had printed a colour copy of the image, and it was now in Alison's bag.

"You promised," said Jack. "You don't say anything."

"I promise," said Alison as she walked towards the door. She already had a mobile in her hand, and when she opened the door and walked into the outer office, she found Cindy sitting at her desk. Alison looked behind her to see Jack hovering nervously.

"Do you have a pen and a piece of paper?" Alison asked. Cindy pulled a piece of A4 from a ream on her desk and handed it to Alison along with the pen she had been using.

Alison lent over and started writing.

"We had a deal," said Jack from behind her, his voice slightly frantic.

"We did," said Alison as she wrote a message, under which she wrote the name and contact details of an employment solicitor she had met in Krav Maga class. "I said I wouldn't speak to anyone." She passed the paper back to the PA. "And I have not."

And with that, Alison turned and walked out of the hut. The screaming started before she even reached the gate.

EIGHT

She was lovely. Of that there was no question.

He drank his overpriced coffee and looked at her some more. God, he wished he had been able to wear one of the new suits - that would impress her. But Spencer had only his lunch break, and there was no way of stashing the suit and changing in time. The surveillance reports had noted that she often spent lunchtime at the Starbucks over the road from the PR company where she worked. Spencer had waited outside on the off chance that she would turn up, and when he saw her his heart skipped a beat. The location was lousy, however, and by the time he had got from Thames House and waited, he had less than five minutes to look at her. It would have been longer, but the staff had taken so long to serve him. It annoyed Spencer. How fucking difficult was it for foreigners to pour coffee?

They had tapped Ms Constance's phone at work but hadn't learned anything of the whereabouts of her ex. She had mentioned him numerous times in private calls, though, and when she expressed her worries for the biker, Spencer felt jealous. It was idiotic. Why was he acting like this? He didn't have time for such foolishness. Not for the watching or the waiting and certainly not for listening to her secretly recorded conversations, something he had been doing at every available moment. But he liked to hear her voice. He had started playing the tapes as he fell to sleep. It helped with the nightmares.

They still hadn't found the biker, and it was causing concern. The Russian paying the bills was looking to him to take the necessary action. He paid well, and Spencer certainly had no wish to find out what happened if the man was disappointed. The Emissary had phoned him again earlier in the day, pressing for updates. The man had proved useful, but Spencer was worried that he failed to understand their respective positions. The Emissary was no more than a gofer - a very useful gofer to be sure but one that increasingly seemed to be having ideas above his station. The Russian had made it clear that Spencer would be in charge and the Emissary was just there to assist. He thought again of that meeting with the Russian and tried to recall the precise words that were used. Those words would be his artillery should he need to lay down the law.

Spencer considered the decision he had made all those weeks ago. It had been a courageous move for certain, and not one that he had undertaken lightly - but then, risk pays.

Spencer was a great fan of FDR. He admired the pragmatic decisions the man had taken. Spencer often thought that the offer that he had made those few weeks ago was one that FDR would have considered in his position. Although if he was honest with himself, he would have to accept that Roosevelt probably wouldn't have provided the whereabouts of a DEA informant to the notorious trafficker about to be endangered by the secrets being offered. In fairness, nothing had ever been proved against the Russian, and everyone was, after all, innocent until proven guilty. That the Russian had not been found guilty was, however, largely due to the fact that his main accuser, a man named Vasquez, had been shot at close range through the head.

The coroner in the Vasquez case had ruled on an open verdict. The gun used was found in the deceased's right hand, so there was the possibility that it had been suicide. Questions had been raised, however, when people realised that Vasquez was left handed. Spencer had learned his lessons from that one. If someone was going to be suicided in the future, it would be done in such a way that no one would ask questions. The fact that Spencer had only been 99.9% successful the next time out was still playing on his mind.

The informant had been Spencer's first killing. He didn't actually pull the trigger - that would have been stupid - but he had commissioned the work. Spencer hadn't lost much sleep afterwards. In reality, he didn't know what the big fuss was. It was just Darwinism, plain and simple. Animals in the jungle killed each other all the time and it was not seen as anything wrong. It was nature. Well, it was natural in humans, too. Those that were strong took out those that were weak. Some slimeball was assassinated - and so what?

Spencer knew that life was no more than a dance marathon, the dancers spinning around one another. The dance went on until one dancer started to flag - and when that happened the flagging dancers were taken out of the game. Vasquez had known the dance, and he had danced well for a number of years, but he had flagged. He had got fat and lazy. He stopped being careful, and as a result he was arrested with a shipment of coke. He hadn't even subcontracted. He would have gone down for twenty plus years. He was vulnerable, and the DEA knew it. So they put pressure on, and he caved. He'd had solid evidence that would have been difficult for the Russian. Spencer had seen the opportunity when the case had come through his office.

The Americans had shared information with MI6, and Spencer had knowledge of the players, so he had been seconded over to his old employers and sent to Washington to interview Vasquez. He was everything Spencer thought he would be and so much more. Drug smugglers in TV were always so cool. It was a lie. They were vicious, certainly, but most of them were about as dumb as they came. Their success was based on pure strength.

Spencer admired that. Strength was good, but it would have been so much more effective in the hands of someone who may have read a book once. It was fair to say that Spencer took an immediate dislike to Vasquez the moment he met him. That was not uncommon; he was a drug smuggler, after all. But it was more than that - there was an arrogance to the man that had really got under Spencer's skin. Maybe it was at that point that he worked out what he would do, or maybe it was later when he got back to civilisation and thought it through. All he knew was that he had made the decision. MI5 had passed him over for promotion too many times. They were to blame. It was naive of them to think that he wouldn't look for alternative employment.

Spencer would get the life he deserved, and Vasquez would get the death he deserved. It was win-win. The Russian would carry on in business - but then he was still dancing strongly, wasn't he? Spencer knew that even if he was taken out of the game, another would replace him instantly. That person would undoubtedly be Russian. They were always Russian. Men who had been born at the right time and place.

Spencer was using his surveillance training - looking without seeming to be looking. It was difficult, though. He had to fight to take his eyes off her.

Across the café, she pulled a mobile from her bag and dialled a number. Spencer wondered who she was phoning. He would, of course, be able to find out very soon. Maybe he would let her conversation take him away to sleep. He hoped it was a happy conversation, maybe a friend, or her family. Life was bearing down on him, and he needed to know she was okay.

He looked at his watch. He hated leaving her, but he had a meeting for which he was already going to be late. Spencer stood, gave her one last furtive glance, and went for the door.

He joined the crowd on the busy street and began walking away as quickly as he could. But then he heard a voice calling "excuse me." He recognised the voice from the tapes, and when he turned he saw Sally Constance smiling at him.

"I think you left this," she said, raising her hand. She had something in her palm. It took him a second to realise that it was his mobile.

Spencer felt his pocket, and indeed his mobile was not there. He replayed his actions. He had put his phone on the table. That was strange - through years of intelligence training, it was not something he had ever done.

Spencer stared at her for a moment.

"Er, thank you," he said as he took the phone from her. In doing so, his finger brushed tantalisingly against her palm.

"Not a problem," she said before turning and walking away.

Spencer watched her walk back into the café, and his heart ached.

. . .

Alison looked at the shelves. She hadn't seen so many geek toys since the television programme Tomorrow's World had finished - and at least most of those inventions had the decency to never go into production. Manson's shop was unlike any other Alison had seen. Where usually a clear high-street presence was seen as vital, this place was hidden away in a nondescript building facing Clapham Common. In terms of location, the rent must have been huge, which made it even stranger that Manson seemed to be doing everything he could to dissuade custom.

She had only found the shop by sending an email to the address on the business card that Manson had passed her at the conference. He had phoned her back within five minutes, and only then did he give her the address.

When she arrived at the locked shopfront, an LED sign above her head had illuminated. The words spelt out in red asked her to state her name loudly and clearly. By the side of the sign, an unhidden camera pointed down, a message as blatant as the illuminated words. Only when Alison had stated her name did the door click open.

Alison still wasn't sure that the man would be able to help. He had done no more than allude to his profession at the conference, but she didn't have many options. Her friend had asked questions about an impossible murder and after doing so had disappeared. And then there was the deleted CCTV video at the building site. To Alison, it certainly seemed that she was in the midst of a conspiracy, and if that was the case, Manson was the closest thing to an expert she knew.

Manson's shop was set out like a small independent bookstore. Shelves lined the walls, and tables took the centre floor space. Across each were a range of cameras and listening and tracking devices. On the table stood a large spider-like drone, four raised propellers at each corner. Alison couldn't help thinking that for a man fixated on an all-seeing government, he seemed quite all right with selling the tools of their trade.

"That's a great product," said Manson as he walked up behind her. "Easy to fly and gets great video. You can put a heat-seeking camera on there if you want. I sell those, too." Manson pointed to the devices on the shelves. "We have listening equipment and hidden cameras." He pointed to the shelf on the other side. "Specialist cameras and trackers."

"And who is your usual customer?" asked Alison.

Manson considered the question. "A range of people."

"Because, no offence, I can't help thinking that this kit would be most of use to stalkers and your garden variety perverts."

Manson smiled. "The government and big companies already have the equipment. I am just levelling the playing field. There is nothing that takes away power more from those who watch us than knowing that they too are being watched. You said you had a photo?"

Alison pulled the photo out from a manila folder and handed it to him.

"It's out of focus, but it looks to me that you are investigating someone from the Darby and Joan Club?" said Manson.

"He looks a little older than most burglars, but we know that he broke into the building site and with at least one other got through a heavily locked cabinet and the security on a video storage system. He then proceeded to delete video from a specific period of time before putting everything back in a way that nobody noticed the incursion."

Manson laughed. "My father can't even work the DVD player."

"Can you make the picture clearer?"

"Maybe."

"Like CSI?"

Manson looked at her like she was a fool. "CSI is shit!" he said firmly. "Don't get me started on the zoom and enhance cliché. It's bollocks. Can't be done."

"So what are you going to do?"

"Follow me."

He led her to a room at the back of the shop. A desk with a top-of-the-range laptop sat amongst boxes of papers. In the corner was an unmade camper's bed, which looked like it had recently been slept in. Manson saw Alison looking at the mess.

"Sorry, cleaner's day off," he said. "That was a lie by the way, I don't have a cleaner. The papers are here because I don't trust that." He pointed to the laptop.

"You don't trust your laptop?"

"I don't trust any computer."

"Impressive machine for one who doesn't trust computers."

"Most of my business is done online. Those that do business with me generally don't want to be watched. It's rather ironic when you think about it." He moved to the scanner next to the laptop and placed the photo on the glass. "Let's see what you have then, shall we?"

The fuzzy photo image appeared on the laptop screen.

"Now let the magic begin."

Manson hit a couple of keys, and the image slowly came into closer focus. It was far from perfect, but the balding man in the picture was now identifiable - at least by anyone who knew him. Unfortunately, Alison was not one such person, and by the look of Manson, she wasn't alone in her ignorance.

"Now, if this was CSI, I would be going into precise detail as to how that worked," said Manson.

"I really don't care."

He snorted. "Good. It's quite dull."

Alison looked at the photo. It clearly showed what the out-of-focus version had suggested. It was not someone in the first flush of youth. Actually, the guy wasn't in the second flush either. An argument could be made for third flush, but that rather did depend on your flushing scale. He looked sixty easily. Alison had first thought that it may just have been his bald head, but the extra detail now visible showed a face that had been lived in.

"Right, we have a photo. What now?" asked Manson.

"We take it to the police."

"Not yet." Manson's attention was fixed on the screen.

"Why not yet?" asked Alison, turning her attention to Manson.

"Our friend has a tattoo."

He pointed to the screen. The bald man was leaning down with his arm outstretched to tie his shoe. Just visible under his black T-shirt was a small section of a red and black tattoo. Alison didn't have a clue what it was, but Manson was staring, fixated by the screen.

"You look like you've seen a ghost," said Alison.

Manson shook his head. "Not a ghost, a spook."

Manson stood and ran over to a shelf where a selection of folders were stacked. He pulled a folder from the bottom of the stack, causing the other folders to come free of the shelf and fall under the power of gravity. The folders clattered as they hit the floor. Manson didn't take any notice, stepping over a file on the way back to the desk.

Manson opened the folder and pulled papers from the top. Alison wondered how he knew where to look. This was certainly no recognised filing system. Manson let out an exclamation, and he pulled from the bottom of the folder a pamphlet. The writing on the front was clearly German.

"I know who is behind this," said Manson.

He opened the pamphlet to reveal a crest of red and black. Inside the crest, an arm held a rifle upright next to a red flag. Alison looked at the laptop screen. She compared the image on the screen to the one in the picture. It certainly looked similar.

"And so who is behind it?" she asked.

"The Stasi," said Manson matter-of-factly.

"The Stasi? As in the East German secret police Stasi?"

"The very same, or at least a fan."

"Are there a lot of fans out there?"

"You would be surprised. Although if he were Stasi, that would explain his age."

Alison looked at the pamphlet. "So, you are telling me that our case of autoerotic asphyxiation is actually a case of mass conspiracy carried out by 1970's secret police, and my best friend has been captured and possibly killed because he found out about it?"

"I have heard of stranger things."

"Really?"

He thought about it. "Actually, no. That's a lie. This is the strangest thing I have ever heard. And I am a fan of slightly mad conspiracies."

Alison smiled. "That's why I came here. I needed an expert. Don't suppose you can tell from the picture how exactly they managed to kill a man without showing up on video, do you?"

He shook his head. "Afraid not. But I may know someone who can assist with the identification of our out-of-time man."

NINE

Alison looked at the pictures on the wall. The imagery was brutal; the haunted eyes of young and old alike stared back at her from some bleak, near-forgotten time. Many pictures showed cramped interrogation rooms, the machinery of torture apparent. Another picture showed the face of a young child, his raised arms showing the scars that had been inflicted to gain information. The images were powerful, of that there was no doubt.

Alison turned away from the displayed photos and turned her attention to the gallery. A few people were wandering around taking in the photos. A gallery of 20th century torture was never going to rival Disneyland as a mass tourist attraction, but Alison would have hoped there would be more people interested. That said, would she have been here if David had not gone missing?

In many ways the place was a lot like Disneyland. The pictures on the wall, a demonstration of the hidden darkness that lay behind "civilised" society. It was just in this version the people in uniform weren't unemployed actors.

Alison suddenly saw the woman she had come to see. Although she had never met her before, Manson had given a near photo-worthy description. She was probably seventy, with long silver hair. Her eyes were a deep blue that seemed, at least to Alison, to hold a wisdom within. They didn't, of course, that was just Alison projecting because of what Manson had told her of the woman. Yet she unquestionably did have an inescapable presence.

Greta Weisch looked around the gallery, her eyes searching. Alison put up her hand in a faint wave. Greta smiled and walked towards her.

Manson had given Alison the potted biography. Greta Weisch had been a writer in the old East Germany. She had a handful of awards to her name. But then she had written her most famous work, a novel that was seen as being critical of the East German government, and she had found herself under surveillance. She wasn't allowed to send the work out of the country but managed to smuggle it through a series of friends. When the government found what she had done, she was arrested and held without trial for twelve years.

Her novel was viewed as a masterpiece by the world. It brought attention to what was happening in East Germany, and Greta became a cause célèbre for Western critics. But it was the effect on her countrymen that was most important. It inspired them. When the wall came down, she was released and set about telling the story of East Germany through the people that lived there. Five years later, she set up a gallery to recognise world torture and oppressive governments. And now, many years later, a handful of people were walking around a building in Central London.

Greta smiled at her. "Alison?"

Alison nodded. Greta held out her hand, and Alison took it. Greta's handshake was firm, the handshake of a dissident.

"It is great to meet you," said Greta. "I believe we have a mutual friend. Manson does not make friends easily. If he trusts you, then so do I."

"Are you close?" said Alison, trying to hide the look of surprise on her face.

Greta laughed. "This astonishes you?"

"A little."

"Mr Manson is a man with a few eccentricities, but you underestimate him at your peril. You thought he was a fantasist?"

Alison shrugged. "Maybe."

"You would be right - mostly, at least. I hear you have a photo for me?"

Alison reached into her bag and pulled out the photo. She handed it to Greta. "I was wondering if you knew who that is? Manson thinks he may have been—"

"Stasi," said Greta, interrupting Alison. "He is Stasi. When

101

Manson said you had a photo, I didn't think I would be able to help. It wasn't just a few people. There were over two hundred thousand members of the Stasi, and many thousands more provided them with information. Children spied on parents, neighbour on neighbour, friend on friend. There were some, though, that reached a level of infamy. Over all the pain and suffering, they were the kings. This is one such man."

"What is his name?"

Greta paused. "Tomas Manner - never thought I would see his face again. I prayed I would not. He has aged. Then again, I suppose we all have."

"What did he do within the Stasi?"

"What did he not do? He wasn't famous in those years, except for those unfortunate enough to cross his path. He gained notoriety after the Wall fell. His name started to be passed around by those who had been questioned by him."

"By questioned, you mean…?"

"Torture, sometimes in the way that you may think of it, sometimes in a different way. He was an expert at messing with heads. He could get you to believe anything he wanted. They called him the Mesmerist."

Alison could see that reliving the history was affecting Greta. The poise so evident only moments ago was now deserting her.

"What happened to him after the Wall fell?"

"No one is quite sure. Rumour has it that he used his skills, not to mention reputation, to forge a career in the underworld."

Alison pointed to the tattoo. "He doesn't seem to be ashamed of his previous work."

Greta smiled sadly.

"A man like Tomas Manner wouldn't be. Maybe he believed in what he was doing. Maybe he just liked having the power of God. You scratch the surface of any of these hard men, and you find a pathetic little bully. Some people have something missing. This man is one of them."

"Do you know where I might find him now?"

Greta shook her head. "I didn't even know he was still alive. He hasn't linked with any of the German community here as far as I know. He wouldn't be welcomed. You don't invite someone like him to your party unless you hate everyone else in the room. You want to have a definition of pure evil, it is this man."

. . .

The bald German was pure evil. Mattie wanted to punch the cunt. Mattie Thompson was a man in hate. Any fool could be in love. Love was for pussies. There was no power in love, contrary to the lies of shit songs. Love made you weak, and Mattie had no time for weakness. Being in hate gave you strength. He was going to kill him. This kraut should never have been brought in. They were supposed to be a crack unit, for fuck's sake. Bloody cabbage munchers, the lot of them.

King Cabbage Muncher threw the photo to the Russian,

who grinned at Mattie in challenge as if to say "come and get it". This wouldn't have happened if Banner or the rest of the Brits were here.

Bloody foreigners. You give them an inch and they take a bloody mile. They were supposed to be the best that the KGB, Stasi, and any other commie spy service could offer up. It was no wonder the fuckers lost if this was the way they carried on. It was childish. There was no other word for it. Mattie didn't know much about communism - he had only been a baby when it had ended - but the evidence displayed in this room seemed to indicate that the whole system worked on the basis of "tag, you're it" mixed with a portion of "you smell" and a bit of "scrap, scrap, scrap". Mattie was a whole generation younger than these sad fucks but was easily the most mature. He was on the playground again, and it pissed him off. Mattie always lost in the playground of life.

Mattie moved towards the Russian, who was now grasping the framed picture of Mattie's mother in his grubby hands. Cabbage Muncher had stolen the picture from Mattie's locked room. Mattie would have been impressed by his lock-picking expertise if it wasn't such a fucking outrage.

"Give it fucking back!" shouted Mattie.

He didn't give a fuck if the tosser was supposed to be ex-KGB. The Russian was so ancient that if his knee didn't give in, it would be a bloody miracle. His knee was likely to give in regardless, because Mattie was planning to take an axe to it whilst the fucker slept.

. . .

Spencer needed to focus. If he could keep on track, he would be fine. The biker would be found and killed, and everyone would be happy. But Spencer's mind kept drifting elsewhere. He knew he should be doing something more effective, but he had given in to the temptation of listening to her voice two hours previously, and now, lying on his bed staring at the ceiling, he imagined she was with him in this room.

He knew it was an illness, and what's more, he knew that this illness had the potential to kill him. He already had to concentrate on two jobs - he didn't have time or energy to waste on a relationship that could never go anywhere.

But then he heard something, and in that something he saw a way to connect with her. The key lay with a random, inconsequential comment in a telephone conversation with a friend. Spencer had a way in.

He began rationalising the situation. She was likely to be the best way of finding the biker. The phone calls and room taps could only give him so much. A personal connection would need to be established to delve further.

Spencer jumped excitedly off the bed. In doing so, he forgot that he had on earphones, and his iPod crashed to the floor. Spencer pulled off the headphones and threw them down next to the iPod. He had things to organise and limited time. He would need a favour - or at least would need to buy a favour.

For a second, he considered contacting the Emissary, although he quickly pushed it from his mind. Spencer was starting to think there was a hidden price for every service offered, and he was beginning to worry that he was running into debt.

. . .

Mattie lay on his bed and looked at the picture of his mother. He wished she was there to advise him what to do. It was not that she was always right. In fact, she had made many mistakes, the most apparent was thinking the bastard she married could be redeemed. She had waited too long to leave, and as a result both her and Mattie had received their share of bruises. Hell, a few broken bones, too - but what's a bit of GBH between family?

Mattie didn't know why Deeko hadn't been subject to the same beatings. He had always been the favourite of his father. Deeko was good at sports in a way that Mattie never was, so maybe that was it? His mother had tried to speak to Mattie about it when she had finally left the Bastard. She said it was her fault, said there was something that she'd done, said that Mattie wasn't to blame. Mattie knew that was rubbish. It was the power the bastard had - he could make you think that black was white at the same time as he was punching you black and blue.

His mother left the Bastard when Mattie was fourteen. The Bastard was down at the pub with Deeko, who was only sixteen but looked older. The landlord knew that he was underage but used to serve him as a favour, because bastards always get favours from like-minded bastards. It's like the Twat Masons.

It was a night like any other. Mattie's mother had a fresh black eye. She had walked into a door again - or at least that was what she would be telling the people in the street.

Even now, he didn't know what made her make the decision she did. He'd seen it in her eyes. Mattie always thought he could see hope in those eyes, although he knew that was silly - they were just eyes, after all. He had filled in the gaps, coloured in the picture with big bold crayons and come up with a memory of hope. It didn't matter, because what happened that day was brilliant. He would always remember the next words she'd said. He often thought about it, especially in moments like this, when the world seemed to be against him. It was the best lesson he'd ever learned. Whatever the circumstances, no matter how bleak the world gets, you can take a stand, make a choice, make life better.

"Pack a bag - only what you need," his mother had said.

Mattie was going to question her, yet there was a determination in her that he had never seen before, and it convinced him to simply do as requested.

He threw a couple of T-shirts and a pair of jeans into a bag, almost forgetting his underpants and socks in the hurry. In truth, there was nothing much he wanted to take. There was only room for sentimental objects when life had some sentiment, and there had been precious little of that in his childhood.

When he got back to the living room, his mother was practically jumping up and down. He had never seen her so animated. She was buzzing around like a bluebottle. Mattie knew he needed to calm her, because he couldn't face her changing her mind. He put his arms around her, held her tight. They hadn't hugged like that for years, as the Bastard had always hated affection in his house. They stayed like that for less than a minute. When most people were asked what their best memory was, they said something like wedding days or holidays, but for Mattie that hug was as good as it was ever going to get. It was the moment his life changed. It was the moment that his mother found her self-worth. At that moment, they both knew that they could do anything they wanted. Unfortunately, God proved to be as much of a bastard as his father.

A month after the divorce had finally come through, she found a lump. Three years later, she was dead. She was happier than she had ever been in those years - well, as happy as any person who was regularly throwing up could be. She had started to lose her hair a few weeks after the treatment started. Six months later, her hair was completely gone. People would always ask how bad things could happen to good people. If there was a God, why did He allow such things? In Mattie's mind there were two options. Firstly, that there was no God, and secondly, God was a right dick.

So as for God's morality, fuck that. Fuck God and his angels.

Fuck the church and fuck the state. Mattie was going to kill, and in doing so, he would shout at God. He would shout at them all. Scream in their fucking faces. The fuckers would see his contempt for their rules.

TEN

David massaged his chained leg. All in all, it had been a strange couple of days. At some other, less thoroughly appalling point in his life, the view he saw through the barred window would have suited him.

It was peaceful, no doubt, but the whole prisoner thing was stifling his ability to properly relax into it. In truth, he would have happily swapped his spacious room here for a cramped jail in Central London, somewhere he could hear other people going on about their lives, where the illusion could be broken that the world was made up of more than prisoner and guards.

His explorations so far had been limited to the twenty-foot by twenty-foot room, restricted as he was by the chain on his leg. It was affixed to the rear brick wall and was long enough to allow access to the totality of the room except the final meter by the door. The shackles had been cushioned with a series of bandages placed between his ankle and the metal brace. David would have been grateful for the padding but for the fact that he couldn't help thinking that the cushioning wasn't for his benefit. They had been tough, all right, but they had always stopped before leaving any sort of mark. They wanted him pristine.

It had probably been three days since they had grabbed him off the street and bundled him into the back of a van. David would have liked to think he would have put up a better fight, but when it had happened, he had been too shocked to do anything, at least for the first few seconds. And a few seconds was all they needed. His face had been covered with a black sack. As he felt the vehicle move, he had the foresight to try and remember noises and changes in direction, but then that was rendered worthless by the needle pushed into his arm.

He had woken on the bed in the corner of the room with the chain on his leg. It was daylight. David's watch had been removed. Whilst he knew that night and day had come and gone twice since, any estimate of what day it was exactly would have been guesswork, as he didn't know how long he had been unconscious.

It was when he woke that he had first seen his jailers. David wished they had covered their faces, but they didn't. Whilst masks may have produced prima facie - or lack of facie - scariness, at least their wearing masks would signify that there was some chance of being returned home safely. These men weren't in the slightest bit worried that he would be able to identify them later. It seemed clear that they weren't expecting this to come to trial, and that was something that worried David more than anything in his life. It was even scarier than turning thirty.

The room that had been his home for the past few days was dated, with flaking paint and a line of damp circling the wall. Although there were bars on the window, he did at least have a view. That was either kind or sadistic - evidence up to this point would seem to suggest the latter. Outside, the woodland was overgrown and wild. It was clear that the building hadn't been used in a long time.

The iron bed had a mattress that proved to be thin and uncomfortable. There was a small circular table and a chair. An old dressing cabinet stood against the far wall, and on the opposite wall was fixed a large mirror. David wasn't sure if the mirror was for his benefit or was instead some psychological torture, forcing him to see what he would look like without showering for days. The answer, as it turned out, was not good. David had never felt the need to grow a beard, always imagining that it would make him look like a pervert - or worse, a geography teacher. He wasn't wrong.

The mirror was nothing compared to the bucket, though. He had never been imprisoned before. Whilst it would have been a lie to say that he had never done anything criminal - he did, after all, have three points on his licence - he had never done anything criminal enough to risk having to slop out on a daily basis. Well, that's what being good gets you - held in chains and shitting in a bucket.

David had never been the angriest of people, but he was beginning to think that now was the perfect time to take it up. Maybe it served him right for asking questions. But the question he was asking seemed such a long shot it was inconceivable that it would lead here - wherever here was. Part of him still felt that they had got the wrong guy. But the trained kidnappers, the injection, the room - everything pointed to bad guys with a big budget. What was the alternative?

If they were holding him hostage for payment, they really hadn't done their homework. He was an actor, and thus skint, as were most of those who would have been bothered enough to pay to get him back. He had thought it was a case of mistaken identity for a while, but when he had tried to express the wrongness of their assumptions, he had been punched in the stomach, at which point he figured that really wasn't an arena for debate.

Every piece of evidence led to the conclusion that these guys really were after him, and unless they were particularly militant theatre critics, upset about an updated version of King Lear, for which the people of Kennington had not been ready, then it had to be the magazine. He thought about Alison. Had they captured her too? He had only seen his room could it be that she was being held elsewhere in the building? But he knew that if Alison were there, he would have heard the shouting. That calmed him. He wondered if she was looking for him.

Much as he enjoyed working with Alison, he had to admit

113

that there were not too many stories they had cracked that would lead to the full-out conspiracy bastardry that he had encountered. In fact, there seemed to be only one option, an option that only a few days earlier had seemed like the delusions of a grief-stricken woman.

Colin Trent was murdered.

There was a part of David that felt like laughing. Sure, he had worked out a way that it could theoretically have been done, but even as he had done so, he had ruled it out. It was just so grandiose. If they hadn't bundled him into the back of the van, he would have put it down to his overactive imagination. But the fact was, they now held him captive. David had solved an impossible murder. He was no nearer to understanding why that murder had taken place, but in terms of how they did it, that was all wrapped up. Ten points to him. Bit of a bugger that it was likely to get him killed, really.

He heard movement behind the door, a rattling of keys. It was a sound he had heard numerous times since he had been brought here, and every time it made his stomach lurch. He knew that it was probably just another routine visit, but one of these times it wouldn't be, and although he hated being a prisoner, it was clearly preferable to whatever changes lay in his future. David, at least at this particular moment in his life, had become a big fan of the status quo - and he wasn't talking about the band.

The door opened, and the ginger-haired guard poked his head around the door and fixed David with a gaze. Whilst he had been relatively well looked after, he had formed an impression of his captors. It was untrue to say that he had favourites, but there were, at least, ones he hated less. There appeared to be three of them, but as he had not been provided with a tour around his new abode, there could have been a cast of thousands, although if that were the case the others must have been mute. The guards had not spoken a single word to him since he'd been brought here, but in those moments when the door was closed and he disappeared from their thoughts, the sounds of three alpha males vying for supremacy was evident.

The ginger guard pushed through the door with a tray of food in his hand. David had watched a lot of television when he was a free man. It was his vice. He loved the detective procedurals most. He had no idea how many times in those programmes talk of the stomach contents of the deceased had been used as a plot point. He had never given it too much thought, but now he couldn't help but wonder if one of the trays of food for which he was so grateful would be examined by a forensic examiner in the next few days. Quincy doesn't seem so entertaining when you are the potential corpse.

The guard laid the tray on the table. He took a cursory look towards David, his eyes checking that the chain on his leg remained firmly in place, before turning and heading back to the door.

"How long are you going to keep me here?" asked David, unable to withhold the desperation in his voice.

The guard continued walking. David knew that the guard was unlikely to break his habit of silence, but it was worth trying, if for no other reason than to make sure his voice still worked.

David moved over to the table. The weight of the layers of material and the chain caused him to limp. Taking a seat, he looked at the food. A couple of rolls of bread and some form of tomato pasta dish. Whoever these guys were, they clearly were not chefs. David ripped apart one of the rolls and dipped it in the overly watery sauce. He was hungry, and if they were still feeding him, there was hope. That was unless they were trying to kill him with culinary disappointment. Maybe he should offer up his services? They would at least have to give him a longer chain.

The food tasted much as it looked. The meal consumed, David considered lying on the bed. He was tired, but he knew the likelihood of falling to sleep was remote. That said, there wasn't a lot else to do. Maybe he was in a TV experiment on the effects of terror and boredom - Extreme Big Brother.

David thought about Alison. He wondered where she was.

. . .

The same woman now glancing at Alison had been in the queue the last time she was here, as were the majority of the people waiting. Alison should have brought a bag with her to at least give the impression that she was going to the gym,

116

rather than waiting around to accost a fitness fanatic with a taste for fried food. While she had not acclimatised to the early mornings, the chance at getting closer to the answer of what had happened to David made her jump out of bed when the alarm went off at 4.30 am.

There was movement inside the gym, and the rattling of keys signified that the people waiting in line were about to get their fix. The door opened, and the fitness zealots filtered inside, leaving Alison again waiting. Within five minutes, she saw Grant running towards her, his legs pumping up the hill. When he got close, he turned his attention to her, and his head dropped. He stopped running and took the last few paces towards her.

"Really?" he said through lungfuls of air.

"I have a lead," said Alison excitedly.

"And it couldn't have waited?"

Alison smiled. "You don't really want to go to the gym when there is a free breakfast waiting for you down the road, do you?"

"And I'm supposed to go like this?" he said, pointing at his sweat-covered T-shirt.

"They didn't look that fussy when we were in there the other day."

"I have standards."

"Okay. Go in, change, and there will be a full English waiting for you when you get to the café." She smiled and began to walk away.

"And if I just work out and leave you there?"

"Well, that would be rude, wouldn't it?"

"Maybe I feel like being rude."

"More than you feel like getting back at the people at work who put you on this case to waste your time? This is an impossible case, a case that no one could solve, except you."

He sighed in exasperation. "Oh, that's good. Well done."

"See you in ten," said Alison, walking away. "Don't be late. It will get cold."

. . .

Nick arrived just as the food was being served. The early hour meant that it was far quieter than the last time she had been here, and there were only two other displaced souls in the café. Nick had changed into a suit, which Alison presumed must have been stored at the gym. She let him finish his breakfast and then ordered two more coffees.

"Let's get down to business," said Alison.

Nick sighed.

Alison reached into her pocket and pulled out the printed photo of the building-site burglar. She handed it to Nick, who angled it towards the light for a better look.

"It's a dreadful photo," said Nick. "He's out of focus."

"He wasn't snapped at a photo shoot."

"I should think not. He's not going to be able to sell clothes to anyone. He's old and blurry," said Nick, smiling at his own

118

joke.

"His name is Tomas Manner. He was a Stasi officer in the day. Those who knew of him talk like he's some kind of devil."

"Can he turn invisible and walk through walls?"

"This photo was taken from the building site on the day Colin Trent was murdered. There were no workers on site that day, and the foreman confirmed he was not one of his."

"So he was trespassing. Probably sleeping rough."

"The video showed two men in the office. This was the only one who was identifiable, but in a short period of time, they managed to break the key code to a secure cabinet, get past the password-protected login of the computer, and delete four hours of recording before putting everything back in such a way that no one noticed they had even been there."

"But even if there were a whole army of Stasi officers on the building site that day, they still couldn't have got into the flat without been seen by the video cameras. There were three on the way into the building, and the nosy neighbour had the camera on the outside. Four cameras, all showing precisely nothing."

"So you don't think it's strange?"

He fixed her with a stern look. "Didn't say that, did I? It is obviously strange."

"So what can we do?"

"When did this become we?"

"Just think about those people at the station and the look on their faces when you solve this. You can be a star," said Alison firmly.

"I don't want to be a star."

"But you want to prove them wrong."

Nick paused in thought. "I don't know anything of the Stasi, but I may know a man who does."

"You have a contact in the Stasi?"

"I worked for Special Branch for a couple of years. There is a chance that Mr Manner is under observation, although he would stand more of a chance if he was thirty years younger and Muslim. I can speak to someone."

"Special Branch?" asked Alison.

"More like people that Special Branch deal with."

"You mean spies?"

He smiled. "Reduce your excitement. Most of them are really dull. The person I am thinking of is both dull and arrogant, but he has an interest in this area. Boring people always have hobbies. If anyone knows who this Mr Manner is, he will."

"So who is this man, then?" asked Alison.

He shrugged. "Not a clue."

Alison looked at him, her eyes asking the question.

He continued. "They are not big on real names. I always knew him as Simon Brown, but he never pretended that it was his real name."

"Can we trust him?"

"As much as we can trust anyone in the Secret Service. If you want answers I can't think of anywhere else to go."

Alison smiled. "Make the call."

ELEVEN

David looked at the image in the mirror. It wasn't a pretty sight. He had never been the sort of man who was obsessed by the way he looked, but the circles he kept did often require some understanding of queer sartorial elegance. Even the worst-kept slob would have been shocked if they looked at his reflection.

His hair had become lank. He hadn't been able to wash. He stank, or at least he thought he did; it was difficult to tell over the stench of the waste bucket, which had not been changed for over a day. He was hungry, tired, and fed up. He had often wondered how he would deal in this sort of situation. Actually, that was a lie, he had never imagined this sort of situation, but he had mentally played out several other less depressing scenarios. He had always felt he would cope well. He would be calm and confident. He would lead, and others would follow. That reality hadn't exactly worked out as he had imagined. It had to be said that David was failing his very first proper emergency with flying colours, and those colours were yellow and smelt of shit.

He wondered what Chris would think of him if he could see him this way. He had dreamed of him the previous night. Chris had looked as he did when David had first met him, before the ravages of chemo had taken hold. When he awoke, it had taken a few seconds before David realised that Chris was gone, but when he did the pain of loss hit once more in his chest.

Dave unbuttoned his shirt and pulled the chain from his neck. Attached to it was the diamond wedding ring that had belonged to Chris's grandma. The ring had been handed to Chris in the old girl's will, with instructions that he hold it until he met the right girl. It was safe to say that Chris's grandma's gaydar needed work. Chris had given the ring to David in his final days, when he was bedridden and weak. He had slipped away soon after. David liked to think that if Chris's grandma was still alive, she would have approved of the gesture. The moment David had first awoken in the room, he had felt for the chain, and the relief he felt on feeling the ring still there made him forget about his predicament. At least until he saw the bars on the window.

He looked at the heavy chain on his leg. He had practiced a little escapology in his time in his stint with the magical bitch from hell. It was part of her set and was always more of an audience pleaser than the card tricks. The truth was that most escapology relied on showmanship and mechanics rather than any great skill. What the audience never realised was that the card trick that they dismissed so quickly required years of practice to develop the required muscle memory needed. David never considered himself to be the best magician's assistant. For him it had been a means to an end. He really wanted to be the one front and centre. He was, after all, an actor, and as such a born show-off.

On stage, this situation would have been solved in a matter of seconds by a hidden key in the mouth or a bogus shackle. David knew that his chain was not a prop, there was no key in his mouth, and the shackle was firm. The padding between his leg and the lock did provide an opportunity, as a couple of inches to either side could be freed up by cutting away the material. He could use the knife from the next meal to do that.

David didn't consider the men holding him to be idiots. He was aware they would have worked out that their captor slipping his chain was a possibility. But then they also knew that even if he did, he still had to get past a locked door and three hard bastards with guns.

The chain was far more of a mental barrier than a physical one. It was about power. They had it, he did not. Unfortunately for them, they hadn't considered one vital fact, and it was a fact that was going to bite them in the arse. If they had seen him on those cruises, they still wouldn't have realised. They would have remembered a middling female magician, and they may have remembered her male assistant, who was cut in half before the intermission. What they wouldn't have known was that the assistant was in disguise. For this man wasn't truly a magician's assistant, but rather the greatest magician the world had ever known. No chains could hold David the Great.

There were footsteps behind the door. From what he could work out from the light through the window and the feeling in his stomach, his captors had kept a regular timing with feedings. They were regimented, creatures of habit. Their stature and strength had led him to believe that they were probably ex-military.

The door rattled, and the scar-faced guard poked his head through. He seemed the most reasonable of all his captors. The evidence for this was limited, but it was human nature to look for a pattern. He seemed to be the leader of the group, and this was the first time he had brought the food. David's stomach lurched as the fear that had subsided reared once again. Scar Face brought in the tray and laid it on the table.

David looked at him. Was this it? If the leader was here, was the status quo about to be changed? Scar Face stared back in silence. David waited, silently praying that he would have another few hours. But he knew he had left it too late. He could have escaped earlier, but now any control he may have had was gone. He had been a fool to expect that they would just release him. He knew what they looked like.

David prayed for the man to leave. Just turn and walk back through the door. If he did that, then this would be his moment. But then Scar Face spoke.

"Bon appétit," he said before turning and walking through the door, jangling the keys in his hand as he left.

But what Scar Face didn't know was that he had turned the key on David the Great, a man that no lock could hold. David the Great waited in the way that a magician did when the cage was being closed. Just before the silk was thrown over, that was when the magic took place.

Close the door. Turn the key in the lock. Make sure the lock is secure. Are you happy? Content that the man in the box is chained? Confident that the box is secure? You have looked at the front, back, and sides, examined the top and the bottom. There are no trap doors. No moveable window panels. Now you know with certainty that escape is impossible. Now be amazed as David the Great gets free of the chains, gets past the locked door and the three armed men. You will believe magic is possible.

And when the door was closed, and when the lock was turned, and when the footsteps of the guard had moved away, David the Great was left alone. He looked at himself in the mirror. The amazing magician had disguised himself as down and out, but his long scraggly hair and dirty face existed simply to fool you. All part of the show, ladies and gents. And as David the Great looked at that image in the mirror, he smiled and whispered just one word, "Abracadabra."

And with that, he disappeared.

. . .

Spencer was feeling pleased with himself. He had obtained every item on his seemingly impossible shopping list and only had to work through the night to do it. Ordinarily he would have been exhausted, but the fact that he was about to see her imbued him with an energy that broke through the fatigue.

Spencer really couldn't understand why the ex-KGB man sitting in the wheelchair was complaining. He was by far the oldest of the collective in the hotel and really looked like a man who would appreciate being able to take the weight of his feet. Spencer had been pushing the old man for ten minutes and had ordered him numerous times not to say anything when they contacted the target. Yet the old Russian really didn't require words to express his anger. It was like pushing around a stroppy, prematurely aged teen. Spencer had told him this was important work and it could certainly be argued that that wasn't a complete and utter lie.

Spencer had been forced to take the day off. There was no way he could have made it from Thames House in time to be where he needed. He had, for the first time in his life, pulled a sickie - and it felt good. He had coughed several times when speaking to the office in a gravelly voice and was pretty certain he had pulled it off. In fact, so easy had it been that Spencer was already planning being sick in the future. His time at MI5 was limited, and a few sick days weren't exactly going to stand in his way in his newly chosen career.

In the wheelchair, the Russian changed slouching positions once more. He really was old. Next time Spencer was going to go for a better mix of recruits. More youthful energy and less rheumatism was the way forward.

Spencer continued to push the ex-spy down the residential street. It was almost time, and she was always on time. He liked that about her.

And then, punctual as always, he saw her walking towards him.

"Right. We are on," said Spencer to the ex-spy, who stared back at him with contempt.

Spencer fumed through gritted teeth. He pushed the wheelchair along the pavement towards Sally Constance. She was distracted, her eyes focussed towards the ground, oblivious to the world around her. He looked towards her, ready to make eye contact, to smile. "What a coincidence," they would say, and she would laugh. But without making eye contact, she passed the grinning Spencer and kept walking. Spencer was lost for a moment, but then he turned.

"It's you," he blurted.

Sally may have been concerned when she first turned, but seeing the grumpy old man in the wheelchair, she relaxed. She smiled at Spencer, clearly trying to work out where she had seen man before.

"You saved my phone yesterday," said Spencer.

"The café," replied Sarah. "Yes. Er, hi."

Spencer stared at her for a moment longer than he should have and collected himself.

"We're lost. You don't know where there's a park around here, do you?"

"Not far. I'm going that way. I can show you."

"That's very kind of you," said Spencer, knowing full well where she was heading. He struggled to turn the wheelchair around, but the Russian was deliberately moving his weight to make manoeuvring as difficult as possible.

It took only five minutes to reach the park, and for Spencer those moments had flown. She was wonderful. Spencer told her how they had agreed to meet a friend of his father's in the park, and they had chatted comfortably along the way. He moved the conversation on to his love of art, and they had laughed that they had the same passions. When they reached the park and were about to split up, Spencer made his play.

"Actually, I have a spare ticket for the Henri Matisse exhibition at the Tate. I can't go, unfortunately. Would you like to have it?"

Her face lit up. "I was trying to get a ticket! They were sold out."

Spencer reached into his pocket and passed her a ticket. It had a face value of five pounds, but Spencer had paid close to two hundred for a pair. He had even travelled south of the river to collect them.

"Here you go," said Spencer. "Seems a shame to let it go to

waste. It's the least I can do to repay you."

Sarah smiled in gratitude, and Spencer's heart combusted.

When she had said goodbye and left, Spencer wheeled the grumpy Russian to a bench by the swings. He took a seat and smiled the biggest smile of his life. Spencer knew that nothing could ruin this feeling.

And then his phone rang and instantly proved him wrong.

. . .

Alison and Nick stood in awkward silence under jaundiced lights. The subterranean car park was empty, and any sound echoed around the concrete walls. The spook had fixed the venue, and it was clear the man had seen All the President's Men too many times.

The meeting had been set for eight, and now it was half past and still there was no sign of the famous Mr Brown.

And then a bell chimed. The recognisable sound of the lift.

Across the car park, the lift door opened, and out stepped an overweight man in a long black coat. The man walked slowly towards them, and as they stepped forwards to meet him, he smiled.

"Good to see you again. You look well," he said, looking at Nick.

"Thanks for meeting with us. This is Alison."

Alison held out her hand, and the man grabbed it and shook. He smiled at her. It was a smile intended to show friendliness while at the same time asserting authority.

"Simon Brown," said the man. Then he gave a look that showed this was clearly an alias.

"We need your expertise," said Nick. "Ex-Stasi officers."

"Bit before my time."

"But not outside your area of expertise?"

Brown nodded, accepting the fact. "An area of only personal interest."

"A hobby?" asked Alison.

Brown smiled. "Some men play with train sets. I am a nerd. I take my job too seriously. It's a flaw."

Alison reached into her bag and pulled out the photo. "We are looking for this man."

She handed the photo to Brown, who made a point of examining it carefully.

"His name is Tomas Manner. He is ex-Stasi," said Alison.

"You know this how?" asked Brown.

"We have spoken to someone who knew him. A person who lived through that time and suffered at this man's hands."

"Do you know him?" asked Nick.

Brown made a point of examining the picture closely again. "I don't believe I do. Anyway, even if I did, I'm not sure what you expect me to do. Many people were in the Stasi, many did awful things, many did not. The world is not a simple place, and those were not simple times. We can't arrest the man for his past legal affiliations, no matter how reprehensible those affiliations may be."

"We think he was involved in a crime," said Alison.

"A crime?"

"The murder of a journalist."

"Which particular journalist?"

Alison paused, at least partly because she didn't trust the man. If Manson was correct about the evil world conspiracy, this man would be one of the key foot soldiers. If she was honest with herself, though, it was mostly because she knew what reaction it would provoke.

"Colin Trent," said Alison.

Brown smiled. The fucker wanted to laugh, it was clear. "Colin Trent? Pretty sure he played with himself a little too often, and in ways that were not sanctioned by any health and safety inspector."

"It may have been more complex than the papers suggested," said Alison, fighting to keep the anger from her voice.

Brown turned to Nick. "Do you think it was more complex?"

"We do," said Alison.

"Not wanting to be rude, but I wasn't talking to you," said Brown, looking at her for no more than a second before turning his attention back to Nick.

"Colin Trent?" asked Brown.

Nick thought for a moment. "The case is strange. I thought there was nothing to it, but the more I look…"

"You always were a good copper. If you hadn't a talent for backing the wrong horse, you would have been running Special Branch by now. I can see why you've been distracted,

131

why you want there to be something in this, but there isn't."

"My friend is missing," said Alison angrily.

Brown held up the photo. "And you think this man took him?

"I don't know. But he is the lead that we have, and I intend to follow it up. Even if you won't help us."

"I never said I wouldn't help," said Brown. "I can ask some questions of colleagues who were around at that time. I'm just saying I am not sure I will be able to do anything even if they do know him. East Germany is history. The world has moved on. We won. Now the service is looking in different areas."

"What can we do while you do that?" asked Alison, trying desperately to hide her growing revulsion of this man and his arrogance.

"I would suggest you wait."

"My friend is missing."

"And is there evidence that he was taken against his will?"

"I know him. He wouldn't just leave."

"Alison, my job makes me somewhat of an expert on human behaviour. Enough of an expert to know that very often people do things that seem out of character. People are weird. They fall in love as quickly as they lose that love. They seek excitement and then hide from danger. They vacillate."

"Not David," said Alison firmly.

"Yes David."

"I am not going to wait."

"And what do you intend to do?"

"I will paste this guy's picture online, and when that's done, onto every lamppost, if necessary."

Brown shook his head slowly, as if speaking to a slow child. "If this man has anything to do with this murder or the disappearance of your friend, and you make his picture public, he will go underground."

"Well, I have to do something."

"Why?" said Brown.

Alison looked at him as if he were a fool.

He continued. "You have spoken to the police. Nick is a fine officer. Let the proper authorities handle it. You will simply get in the way if you meddle. And as I said, from what you have told me, I am far from convinced that anything is awry."

"You have twenty-four hours," said Alison. "If you don't find something by then, I am going public."

Brown smiled coldly. "You seem to be under the impression that I am working for you. I am here to consult. As a favour to an old colleague." He turned to Nick. "You agree with me, don't you?" asked Brown, sure of the answer he would receive.

"Not really," Nick replied with a smile. "As you said, the police don't have much to go on at the moment. If it gets to a stage where we do have something to go on, it will probably be too late. If you can get something in twenty-four hours, so much the better. If not, I think Alison would be wise to seek other assistance."

Brown looked at him as if he was speaking in tongues. He clearly felt he had control over Nick, and Alison saw it in his eyes the moment the harsh truth was revealed. She couldn't help smiling.

"I'll see what I can find out."

"Thank you," said Nick. "Let's meet tomorrow."

"I caution you on getting your hopes up. This man may have been observed in the past, but it is unlikely that we are still keeping tabs on him."

"And if that's the case, we have an alternative course of action," said Alison.

"I will phone you." He turned without saying goodbye and walked towards the lift.

"Well, he was lovely," said Alison quietly.

"He's an acquired taste."

"Have you acquired it?"

He shrugged. "Not really."

TWELVE

The guard with the red hair was a man known to both friends and enemies alike as Campbell. His Christian name was a mystery to all but his mother, who having invested a whole two minutes thinking of a suitable name for her newly born son, had concluded that effort so expired should not be wasted. She alone, therefore, had continued to call him Kevin.

When Kevin turned the lock and opened the door, it was with a certain degree of surprise that, instead of a chained man, he saw a loose chain lying on the floor along with the remnants of the leg padding.

Kevin, being a trained soldier, was not a man to panic as many would by this revelation. He knew that the bars on the window were strong, and the fact that he had needed to turn the key in the lock showed that the door had not been breached. This could only mean that the captive was in the room and was hiding in preparation for an attack. Kevin did for a second think of calling down to his colleagues for assistance but instead steadied himself with the knowledge that he was a trained killer and could more than handle the situation.

At the current count, Kevin had killed eight men in hand-to-hand combat. Only five of those men had been soldiers, and just three of those had been on the enemy side, but the fact remained that not one of those men had come close to besting him.

Confident as he was in his ability, he considered it almost cheating to pull his gun, yet he did so anyway. They had been given strict orders that the captive was not to be marked, but if it came to it, Kevin decided that just for wasting his time, the captive was going to get a slap. He entered the room, sweeping left and right, he checked behind the door - but there was no captive to be seen. Kevin took in the room and watched for movement, but there was none. He looked past the circular table to the bed and wardrobe at the far end of the room. Only two options remained: either the captive was hiding under the bed or he was in the wardrobe.

Kevin moved forward slowly. He kept his finger off the trigger. The gun was as much for show as anything, as the instruction to leave no marks almost certainly included bullet holes.

He walked past the table and first turned his attention to the bed, crouching down and looking underneath. He could see through to the back wall - no one was there.

All other options being eliminated, he turned his attention to the wardrobe. Inside, he knew there would be a man ready to fight. He slowly moved to the door, grabbed the handle, and flung it open. The expected attack never came, mostly because the wardrobe was empty but for a small amount of broken wood.

Kevin was befuddled. He looked around the room, trying to make sense of what was happening. As he did so, he noticed the room seemed different, although he couldn't quite put his finger on why. Something was missing, and it wasn't just the captive.

· · ·

In an average room, in an average flat, on an average street, a man known to Alison only as Mr Brown weighed up his options. As he did so, he listened to a tape. A recording of a woman named Sally. The man known to Alison only as Mr Brown needed to hear Ms Constance's voice again. It calmed him.

· · ·

David ran as fast as he could on legs that felt like rubber. They had been rarely used in the last few days, as the now discarded chain had made excessive movement uncomfortable. The grass was damp, and the soles of his impractical city shoes slipped and slided. His breath was heavy, his lungs bursting. He dared not look back, hoping with every fibre of his being that they were not following.

The exit from the room had been easy. People were never able to see what was right in front of them, and magic relied on those same people never questioning their senses.

The danger had always been once David had escaped from the room. The magical powers of the David the Great only extended so far, and if it came to a man-on-man fight, a nifty card trick wouldn't be much use.

Thankfully, it had not come to violence. As he had estimated, there had proved to be just three jailers, and with the ginger guard confused and searching, just two men stood between David and escape. Fortunately for him, the two men in question seemed to have a liking for Chuck Norris films. They didn't even move their eyes from the TV as he crept slowly past. The movie had been in English, which at least held hope that he was still in the UK.

Now he needed to focus, get to civilisation, and sound the alarm. Unfortunately, when David fled from the building, it became clear that civilisation wasn't going to be easy to find. It had been obvious from his view through the window that he was in a remote area, but he didn't imagine that it would be this remote.

Tall dense trees reached out in all directions. There had been a battle between nature and man, and nature had been victorious. Not a single man-made structure could be seen but for the narrow road that led to the house. The road would obviously be the closest route to where he needed to go, but it was too dangerous. It would only take a minute for them to work out what had happened. The magic of David the Great was about to be revealed, and when the details of the trick were known, the audience would feel cheated. The difference between this audience and all the others he had played were that this audience was armed.

He had only a second to make up his mind. The road was out; they would catch him in minutes. He could run straight ahead, but people always ran in a straight line. He could creep around the house and push through the forest, but that was going to keep him close to the house, allowing more time to be spotted. Left or right? The guards had all been all right-handed, and so David turned left and ran into the dense forest. His legs caught against weeds, and branches brushed against him, scratching his arms and face. But he kept going.

It was ten minutes before his lungs gave in and he fell onto the ground, breathing heavily. The environment looked exactly the same as when he had started. Tall dense trees, harsh terrain.

David had been afforded a few days to consider his position. If this was about Colin Trent, and if he was right about how Trent had been murdered, then it would have taken a lot more than three people. If it was a full-on conspiracy, then more people could be called to track him down. That was if the three guards were going to phone for reinforcements straight away. They had fucked up. He was a nobody who they had chained in a room behind a locked door, and yet they had let him escape. These guys weren't the brains of the outfit. That meant there was a boss. And that meant those guys were in the shit.

David liked to think he understood people, and he knew that they were, at heart, mostly cowardly. No matter how big and strong a person may be, the act of owning up to a mistake made everybody a child in front of the head teacher. Those men would do what they could to track him down, lock him up, and never admit to their failings. That gave David some time, but not much. For all he knew there was an army of knuckleheads just down the road waiting for the call.

He pushed himself up, and keeping his body as low as possible, he moved on. Becoming invisible had been easy - staying invisible would be far more of a challenge. David the Great could help no more. He was on his own, more so than he had ever been before.

THIRTEEN

Spencer was surrounded by the most pretentious people London could provide. He looked over the items of so-called art. He used to do better than that when he was a child with a paint brush and crayons. Everything was spinning out of control. He had almost not come here, but what else could he have done? Maybe seeing her would calm him. But she still wasn't at the exhibition, and he was beginning to lose hope she would turn up at all.

It had been a stressful day in the extreme. First there was the email from Nick Grant. Spencer couldn't believe they were asking him for help in solving the crime that he himself had coordinated. Really, what were the chances? At first Spencer felt they must be on to him, but after thinking it through, he realised that there was probably nothing to worry about. Spencer was known for his interest in East German security services, and Grant knew Spencer. What was most worrying was the fact that they had a photo of his operative. It was another undone stitch.

At first Spencer decided not to return the email. Showing his face would be a dangerous move that was unlikely to have any advantage, but the longer he thought on it, the more he knew he was going to meet them. In meeting them, he would find out exactly what they knew, which would allow him to have control over the situation. His dealings with Special Branch had been infrequent, and what he had seen disappointed him. Nick was the best of a bad bunch, but even he had a restricted imagination most of the time. What's more, the man had a weakness that led him to burn his relationship with Special Branch for good. He was now a blunt weapon.

Spencer was truthful enough to admit he was nervous when he met with them. When that lift door opened, his heart was in his mouth. He half expected to see an armed unit pointing guns at him. Yet he had known that was irrational. He believed that she knew nothing, and in that belief, he had been mostly correct. Importantly, she had no answer for how Trent had been murdered - but then again, what woman would have the imagination to solve that mystery? It was clear that the time was now right to kill the snooper and get Banner and his team back to London.

What they had was no more than a blurry image of an elderly German man. So he was a member of the Stasi when he was younger? So were hundreds of thousands. Never had a state invested so much in the control of its people. It was an achievement that had always impressed Spencer.

He weighed up the options of what to do with Tomas Manner. He could send him home with enough to keep him quiet, but that felt like failure. Even if Spencer did that, it wouldn't stop the woman from posting the picture of him on her website. It was probable that no one would pay attention, of course. In fact, this was the most likely scenario, yet it was noise where there should be silence.

From the early planning it had been clear, Trent would be killed, and no one would question. For weeks, it had seemed that he had achieved the impossible. It was majestic. But now there were questions, and those questions wouldn't go away. They would grow like a cancer. And everyone knew what you do with a cancer: you eliminate it at the earliest stages.

Spencer's phone rang. Every eye in the exhibition turned accusingly towards him. He had been instructed to turn his phone off, but he'd thought surely no one paid attention to that. Yet he still wanted to escape these pretentious arseholes, so he turned away from the substandard art and headed for the entrance. He hit the green button and placed the phone to his ear. It was only a ten-metre walk to the entrance, but by the time he got there his face was red, his heart was racing, and he felt like his legs would give way.

It was a fucking disaster! His guys were supposed to be the best in the business, and they had let an unarmed, chained man escape from a sealed room. Spencer had to take control, but how could he? He was too far away.

And then he saw her. She looked wonderful in a patterned white dress. She smiled at him, surprised obviously that he was there. Seeing he was on the phone, she showed her ticket and walked into the exhibition. He watched her go, and for a second forgot the world was ending.

On the other end of the line, Banner had stopped apologising and moved on to the situation at hand, notably that the ex-prisoner was nowhere to be found and more hands were needed in the search. Did they expect him to hire a minibus? When Spencer hung up, he realised that there was only one man who could help, although the idea of asking for another favour filled him with fear. He dialled the number, and within two rings, the Emissary had picked up the phone.

It took Spencer ten minutes to compose himself after the call. The Emissary had done what Spencer had asked and had never raised his voice. Yet there was something unnerving about the way he had agreed, something cold.

Spencer walked back into the exhibition and looked for her, finding her by a totally awful painting on the wall. She was alone. Part of him felt like running, but instead he walked over.

"Nice painting," he lied.

She turned at him and smiled, but then seeing his face, her smile turned to concern.

"Are you all right?"

It took Spencer a moment to realise what she was talking

about. He should have stopped off on the way to check how he looked. That was what he usually would have done. Spencer always sweated a little when he received bad news. A quick towel down would have done the trick, but he was distracted both by the news and by her. He needed a good excuse. His brain rummaged round for something to say. He fell back to one of the lines he had used when he thought of her last night, where unbeknownst to her they had shared an excessively intimate eight and a half minutes.

"I have had some news about my sister," he said before adding, "She's missing."

. . .

Mattie couldn't believe it. There had been days of waiting with bugger all happening, and now there was a big "all hands to the pumps" disaster, and he was invited. Everyone else on the plane was asleep, but Mattie couldn't. He was too excited.

The call had come in four hours before. Fat Boss had phoned and ordered practically everyone to pack their best boots and head out. Some had refused to go when they heard of the location, but Mattie had been well up for it. He wasn't scared. He didn't know what all the fuss was about. It wasn't like the old commies were in any risk of being new fathers anyway.

Mattie had never been on a helicopter, but now he had, and it was brilliant. And that had been just the start of it. The helicopter had taken them in batches to an airfield. At the airfield was the biggest plane Mattie had ever seen. It was like a building with wings.

Up until recently he had been on a plane only once in his life, when he went with his mother to Tenerife. By then they knew that the cancer was there to stay. She said she wanted him to have a good holiday, the sort she had always wanted for him but could never afford. That holiday was fantastic, but that plane had been nothing like this one. This plane had a giant door that folded down from the rear.

Mattie was surprised that there were no seats, just benches around the outside. There hadn't been any stewardesses giving safety instructions, either, which was probably a good job, because once the plane had thundered across the tarmac, it had taken off almost vertically. All the old guys were scared. They tried to hide it, but Mattie could tell.

Mattie wasn't scared, at least not after the first minute or so. He thought it was the best plane journey ever. But then he remembered the trip to Tenerife again and realised that wasn't the case.

. . .

It was dark, and David was cold. The harsh terrain had turned to mud, and that mud had then turned to swamp. He was now up to his waist in foul-smelling water, and as his feet pushed through weeds and rushes, David realised he had gone the wrong way. The water had got deeper as he walked, and he was beginning to fear it would never bottom out. It was now just one of the fears going through his head. It was a fear running alongside being swallowed by mud and attacked by creatures in the water. The fears had intensified once the sun had fallen. Luckily it was a clear night, and the moonlight allowed him to see for a short distance ahead.

This was not the way he wanted to die, and yet he knew turning back was not an option. They would be after him. He would keep going, pray that the solid ground would return, and that there he would find a glimpse of civilisation.

Those after him would undoubtedly be far more used to this sort of environment than he, but unless they had night-vision goggles, they were going to have to use lights. That would overcome his biggest fear - that he wouldn't see them coming.

David felt very alone. He thought about Alison. He hoped he would see her again.

. . .

Alison looked at the stars. She had lived in the flat for three years and had probably used the garden only four times. It was paved and thus required very little attention—something that was a big advantage to a woman who didn't know plants from weeds. It was a garden that a few days ago she was worried about losing, along with her flat, when the money finally dried up.

Yet now, as she looked at the twinkling dots, the flat and

garden seemed insignificant. David was missing, and she didn't know how or why. She just knew she had to do everything she could to find him.

FOURTEEN

As Mattie stepped over the rough terrain, he looked down the barrel of his newly acquired semi-automatic. Sweeping left and right, as he had seen in the movies, he watched his torch beam reflect off trees and foliage. He had found his calling. Mattie was hunting human prey, and he liked it.

He had arrived with the others at a ramshackle house less than an hour before, and little time had been wasted before the team was out and searching. Mattie knew nothing of his prey, but he had at least now seen a picture of him, which in comparison to the last week seemed like a news bonanza. The man was black, which was a surprise to Mattie. He didn't know how to feel about this new information. Unlike his brother and father, Mattie wasn't racist, and now he, along with twenty other white men, were hunting a black man to slaughter.

In Mattie's head, there was a distinct touch of the Deep South to the whole endeavour, and he wasn't talking about Bognor. Mattie consoled himself with the knowledge that he had been hunting the man before he realised he was black, and on that basis it would, in fact, be racist if he wasn't trying to kill him. Race was complicated, and so Mattie decided to put it out of his mind and just concentrate on putting one foot in front of the other.

He looked again at his new gun. When they had arrived at the house, Banner had opened up the back of the truck to reveal an arsenal of automatic rifles. It sounded strange, especially as all the rifles seemed identical, but Mattie saw instantly the one he wanted to hold. The commies had moved in to collect their weapons, and Mattie feared she would be picked up. Yet when he got last dibs, she was still there waiting for him. When he touched her, the hair on the back of his arms fizzled, and his heart beat faster. She felt substantial in his hands. As he moved his fingers slowly down the barrel, he felt the cold killing metal and knew he would always remember this moment. The moment he fell in love for the first time.

Once they had collected their guns, Banner passed around the photo and told them the job. The man had a twelve-hour head start, but Banner said that he would have to rest, whereas they did not. When he heard this, Mattie wished he had slept on the plane like all the commies. He had been surrounded by snoring on the journey but put it down to the collective age of the commies, which must have been in the thousands, rather than some thought through strategy.

Mattie would deal with the tiredness. At least it was far better than the miserable old fuckers that surrounded him. They didn't look like they were having fun at all. The whole thing looked like a badly organised day out at a retirement home.

. . .

Spencer was dreaming about her when he was awoken by the pain in his hand. His eyes flashed open as he looked around to find the cause. He found the answer in the heavily muscled skinhead at his bedside, who seemed focussed on bending back Spencer's index finger. It was then that Spencer's mouth roused and screamed out in pain - at least until a large callused hand covered his lips and pressed his head back forcibly onto the bed.

Spencer's awaking mind looked for answers, but his brain was too far slumbered to come up with anything. It would take about a second for it to catch up. When the light flooding through his retinas finally reached his brain, he would recognise the willowy man in the background but would not have the same knowledge of the skin-headed muscle dominating the foreground. But he would identify that the guy looked scary as fuck and quickly surmise that he should fear for his life. Luckily for Spencer, his sphincter was better at stirring than the rest of him, and this was the only reason that he didn't

151

shit the bed. It was the only upside to a series of heavy-duty downsides of the first ten seconds of his day so far, but one that, as the day progressed, he would look back on as a real high point.

Spencer struggled to breathe. The skinhead's hand remained over Spencer's mouth, pressing so strongly he feared he was being smothered to death. He sensed movement to his right and saw the willowy man with glasses approach the bed. He was a man that Spencer knew. Spencer turned his eyes, trying and failing to hide the panic contained within.

He watched as the Emissary pulled a chair towards the bed and sat. The Emissary looked at Spencer briefly, and then, pulling the glasses off his nose, began to wipe the lenses. Whilst the Emissary wiped, the skinhead continued to press down. Spencer tried to talk, but it came out as no more than a muted moan. Finally, the Emissary folded the cloth into his pocket and put his glasses back on his face. Spencer would later hate the man for his theatricality, but at this present moment, the act was working, and the effect left him very much in fear of his life.

"Enough," said the Emissary, and the skinhead pulled his hand away from Spencer's mouth.

"You are not going to scream, are you, Mr Townsend? Such an action would be ill-advised. Michael here is well trained but sometimes unaware of his own strength."

Spencer shook his head nervously.

The skinhead stepped back from the bed.

"Why are you here?" asked Spencer, his attempt at presenting a calm demeanour failing.

"Why? Why? Why indeed?" said the Emissary. "It is a fine question, and one that undoubtedly deserves an answer."

The Emissary made a point of looking around the bedroom. "It is a small room you have here. Compact. You like this small room?"

Spencer was silent as he tried to work out just what the hell the man was talking about.

"What difference does it make?" asked Spencer finally.

"A man should be as comfortable in his home as he is in his skin. This is your castle, is it not? Yet the pictures and décor, I do not think are you. The… how you say…pokiness… certainly does not equate to the man who bravely approached my employer all those weeks ago. That man would have a large house."

"You wanted me to keep my job. I have to keep a low profile to do that. I need to blend in. I can't flash my cash and…"

"Ah, it is a disguise. And those pictures on the wall, the art, is that also a disguise? Tell me, are the paintings designed to fool them or to fool you? They are prints, yes?"

"Yes."

"I thought so. Real paintings wouldn't fit in an environment so obviously fake. The question is, Mr Thompson, how real are you? I fear you are no more than a poor replica yourself."

"I don't understand. Can I get up and we can…" Spencer moved to get out of the bed, but his progress was halted by the

Emissary placing a hand on his shoulder.

"Let me clarify. The man who visited my employer claimed to be able to work miracles."

"I did work miracles," said Spencer angrily. "Vasquez is dead. Trent is dead. No one asked questions, it's..."

"But that is untrue, isn't it, Mr Townsend? People did ask questions."

"One person."

"And one person is enough. Now, you sought our help to deal with this person, and that help came at not inconsiderable expense to my employer. And yet you convinced me that this was the best way forward, so we did what was asked. But now our question-asker is no longer under our control."

"It's a blip," said Spencer.

"It is a very big blip. It is a blip that has caused my employer much expense."

"He can afford it."

The Emissary nodded. "True. But it really isn't about the money, is it? You are paid very well, Mr Townsend. Already you have made enough to replace these poor replicas on your walls with the real things. Yet you have not done so. I would really like to think that was down to you feeling that you had not earned the money yet."

"My best men are searching for..."

"Your best men are very old, are they not? You really think they can deal with this situation?"

"They are the most experienced..."

The Emissary shook his head sadly.

"They are old!" the Emissary shouted before instantly returning to his calm demeanour "Sorry, I interrupted you."

"There is nowhere the man can run."

"There are always places to run. It is a question as to whether you can find people on the run."

"Exactly. And due to the location, he is not going to find anyone, is he?"

"I'm afraid your statement simply shows the sloppiness of your research. There are people he can find, and those people need to be made not to listen. This is something I could have arranged, yet you chose not to ask. I really feel that you have a lack of understanding of our respective positions. Did you think I was, as the Americans would say, a gofer?"

Spencer remained silent.

The Emissary smiled. "You did, didn't you? No matter. My position, as long as everything goes to plan, is unimportant. I will be a simple servant, should you wish. But to my employer, I have another role. Do you know what that is, Mr Townsend?"

"What?" asked Spencer.

Suddenly the Emissary tightened his grip on Spencer's shoulder. Bringing his other hand up, he drove his fist into the joint of Spencer's shoulder. The pain was excruciating, and Spencer couldn't help crying out.

"I am the man they send in when people do not live up to my employer's expectations."

Spencer's shoulder was in agony. He tried to squirm away,

but this small man held him fast.

"Do we understand one another?" asked the Emissary.

Spencer nodded his head violently. The Emissary pulled his hand away and again reached into his pocket for the soft cloth. He pulled his glasses off again and started wiping the lenses.

"I hear you took the day off yesterday. You were ill?"

"I needed to make a contact, in relation to the biker."

"Indeed. The biker my employer was assured would be dead by now and is clearly not."

"I thought that his girlfriend may be able to..."

"Your interest in his girlfriend is strange. I hear you have been listening to tapes of her house?"

Spencer considered his response, keen to move the conversation away from Sally as quickly as he could.

"She is our best chance of finding him."

"Is it that, or is it something else, I wonder? I think maybe you were not satisfied with my present to you the other day. Was Maria not to your taste?"

Spencer nodded enthusiastically. "She was wonderful."

"Isn't she? I often partake myself, but I was more than happy to share with a man who had done a good job. That seems such a long time ago now, does it not? This is the way I like to manage, you see. Punishment and reward. Not that I wish for you to think of yourself as a caged dog, you understand. But now things are not going so well, so the rewards get put away, and the punishment must follow, or else how is the dog to learn? Let's pick up our ideas, shall we? And no more sick days, I think.My employer wants a man on the inside of British intelligence, and you really don't want to lose your job."

"But it's too much. I need to have just one job," said Spencer desperately.

"That is just silly talk. In leaving MI5, you would be of little use to us. Trust me when I say that you really don't want to be of little use. It would not be a healthy approach for you. No, simply find and kill everyone you need to find, and kill. And do it quickly - my employer is beginning to lose patience."

. . .

David remained still, like prey fixated on a predator. He had been holding his breath, but being able to do so no longer, he let the air out of his lungs as silently as he could. He'd heard that some animals could smell fear, and he really hoped that wasn't the case, because he was terrified. That said, the stench from his unwashed body was probably hiding any competing scent. As the creature looked towards him, its eyes seemed to look into his soul. It wasn't simply the size and reputation of the creature that scared David, it was the fact that unless wolves had been silently reintroduced into the UK, he wasn't in Kansas anymore.

Since escaping the house, he had become increasingly convinced that once they had rendered him unconscious, they had moved him out of England. The fauna and marshland he had been fighting his way through didn't resemble any of England's mildly contoured fields. Now the large grey creature he was staring at had devoured any hope that this was some out-of-the-way area of Kent.

He had woken when the sun rose, and it was as he was preparing to get moving that he had sensed the creature out of the corner of his eye.

The night had been long, and pain had competed with fear for David's attention. After what had seemed like an eternity of battling through marshland, the water had finally subsided, and firmer ground took its place. As soon as the ground had become firm enough to lie on, David had collapsed in exhaustion. Even though he was soaked to the skin, tiredness had overwhelmed him, and he found sleep far faster than his terrified brain would have expected.

David made it through the night. No lights had shone upon him. No vicious thugs had wandered by and killed him in his sleep. Now he needed to get up and move on. Yet the wolf held his ground, moving neither forward nor away.

David had hoped that the sunlight would give him some idea of where he was, but when he woke, he had been met with the sight of more endless trees and overgrown foliage. It looked no different from the terrain he had escaped into all those hours ago. He worried that he had walked in a circle, and that at any moment he would come across the house from which he'd so recently become unshackled.

He needed to find civilisation. That would be more difficult now that it was clear that he was no longer in England, but even so, there were 7.7 billion people on the Earth, how widely could they be spread? He had to come across someone soon, surely, even if it was someone with a liking for extremely bleak forests. But in order to find that someone, he was going to have to move, which meant that the furry grey danger had to leave. David considered making a loud noise, waving his arms, or just relying on the fact that the way he smelt made it unlikely that even the most desperate creature would want to take a bite. Thankfully, after another few seconds, the animal turned and trotted off, clearly content that David was neither a threat nor suitably edible.

With the creature gone, David pushed himself to his feet. His legs ached more than they had ever done before. His shoes were still wet, and as he placed weight on his feet, the pain caused him to grimace. He tried to bend down to undo his laces but in doing so overbalanced and stumbled to the ground. It was going to be one of those days.

He lay there for a few moments, then turned onto his back and forced his aching body to bend enough to let his hands reach his laces and undo them. He pulled off his black leather shoes. Those shoes, which had looked so good walking down London's Brewer Street, had proved impractical in a battle for survival.

When the shoes were removed, he pulled a sock off each foot and examined the damage. His feet were red and blistered, but neither looked as bad as they felt. The question was whether to put the shoes back on or go barefoot. David looked at the rough ground and made up his mind. The shoes may be wet and badly designed for the terrain, but they would go at least some way to preventing his skin from being punctured. He wished he could have made a fire to dry them, but that was not an option, partially because the wood around him was so wet but mostly because he had only ever seen people lighting fire with sticks on TV and didn't feel that was sufficient preparation to attempt it in practice.

He pushed the wet shoes back on his feet and stood again. They would be after him. He needed to move. And move he did. One painful footstep at a time.

. . .

Alison sat in front of her computer, looking at the magazine's website. She had been devastated when it was clear that the business was over, yet now it seemed of little importance, evidenced by the fact that she hadn't looked at the site since David had gone missing.

But when she awoke she realised that the website that she had ignored might be of assistance. The readership had never been significant enough to sustain a business, but they did at least know David's face and were, by their very nature, people that loved a mystery. Well, here was a nice juicy puzzle for them.

Alison had spent an hour writing the thousand-word story.

She had omitted the details of the Stasi agent as agreed, but she had covered everything else - from the impossible murder to David being missing to the builders that weren't. The article was good if she said so herself. In fact, if they'd had more mysteries like it, maybe the magazine would have lasted.

She read through the item twice, corrected typos where she found them, and then hit the button to post the story, at which point the screen turned white and she was met with an error warning. Alison tried reloading the page but again was met with the white screen. The website was out of service, and Alison couldn't help feeling that the cause was not innocent.

FIFTEEN

Mattie struggled to keep his eyes open. It helped that he was up to his chest in rank water, but the flipside was that he was up to his chest in rank water. The effort to hold his precious rifle above the water was causing intense pain in his arms and shoulders. The worst pain, though, was in his thighs, where his submerged jeans were rubbing against his legs.

All in all, it was nowhere near as much fun as Mattie thought it would be. He wanted to stop and sleep, but that was not an option. The only choice was to keep walking, to place one painful foot in front of the other and press on.

The torch mounted on Mattie's gun picked up King Cabbage Muncher in front of him. The man seemed to be in his element. Mattie did, for a fraction of a second, consider levelling the rifle and shooting the fucker in the back, but on balance, he thought that may be marked down as unprofessional.

Mattie's leg got caught in the weeds again. He kicked forward to release himself. The whole ordeal really was rubbish.

. . .

Spencer had been torn ever since the Emissary and the muscled oaf had left. He so wanted to meet her, but now he felt that his every movement was being observed.

The lie about having a missing sister had come out of nowhere but had proved to be the improvisation of a genius. It had ignited a conversation that had lasted an hour and resulted in an invitation to meet for a drink and talk further. When Spencer turned up to the pub, he found her waiting for him at the bar. She smiled, and even though the captive and biker were still missing, and the Emissary was utilising performance-related agony, that smile made him feel safe.

He was right to meet her. To hell with the Emissary. Spencer was the expert - that was why they had hired him. If they needed to find the biker, this was likely to produce the best intelligence. She also looked fantastic. It was win-win.

The pub was busy, and Spencer had to walk past groups of people to get to her. As he walked, he had time to reflect on the actions he had taken that day. The Emissary had raised the stakes, and Spencer had reacted. He made a call, the consequences of which would transpire over the next hour. He trusted the men he'd put on the case, but he was aware that everything was on the line.

He wished the people in the bar would get out the way. He needed to get to her. She would calm him.

. . .

Alison took a sip of Coke. The pub was empty but for the barman, an old man with a dog sitting at the bar and Nick, who sat opposite her. The suit was gone, and thankfully, so was the leisure gear. He was wearing a plain shirt and trousers, and whilst still not looking the height of fashion, he did at least look like this was the real version of Nick Grant.

Nick had phoned and said that Mr Brown had asked to meet them at this place. It was a grotty old man's pub - the grottiness in question covered the pub, barman, and clientele - even the dog had seen better days.

And yet again, the spook had left them waiting. He was clearly a man who loved to make an appearance.

"He's late," said Alison, as much to restart a conversation that had begun to falter.

Nick nodded. "He never was a man who paid much attention to other people's schedules."

"Thanks for doing this," said Alison.

He sighed. "I just want to stop you waiting outside leisure centres every morning."

"You think Brown will be able to help?"

"Maybe, maybe not. But there is something strange going on, and the bit of me that remains a good copper wants to find out what that strange thing is."

Alison paused, unsure of whether to ask her next question. "Why do they give you a hard time at the station?"

"It's a long story."

"We have time to kill."

"I don't want to talk about it."

Alison nodded her agreement to stop the questioning. She took another sip of Coke and looked over to the door in expectation. But Brown didn't walk through, and the awkward silence engulfed them once more.

"I was in Special Branch," said Nick, not being able to take the silence anymore. "Doing well. Well regarded. A good copper. There was a party. I met someone. A woman. We fell in love. Unfortunately, the woman in question was the wife of the commander."

Alison furrowed her brows. "Not a good career move."

"To say the least. I had to move from Special Branch. It was fine for a few weeks, but the commander in question, as well as having a liking for domestic violence, also had a lot of contacts in the force. It started with looks and quiet asides. Then it got worse. My career is essentially over. Wherever I go, the tentacles of that bastard will follow."

"If you had your time over again?"

He shrugged. "I would do the same thing. She was worth it, and she needed me."

The phone of the desk vibrated, and Nick picked it up and looked at the screen. "Bugger!"

"What is it?"

"Brown. He said he can't make it. Government business. He'll contact us later."

"So what are we supposed to do?"

"We go home. Unless he contacts me again, I say you publish tomorrow."

Nick stood, and Alison followed his lead.

"Can I give you a lift?" he asked.

She smiled. "Thanks."

As they headed for the door, Alison took a mental note never to come to this dive again.

Across the bar, the old man with the dog watched them leave. The man's name was Dimitri Kosco, the dog's name was unknown, as Dimitri had stolen him less than an hour beforehand. Dimitri reached into his pocket and pulled out a mobile.

Outside the pub, the night air hit Alison. There was no parking in the street, and Nick had been forced to park a distance away. They turned right and sauntered along the pavement.

The streets that earlier would have been busy with office workers were now empty. As they walked past an alleyway, there was a muted cry. Nick stopped dead in his tracks. Another cry. A man's voice shouting, "Help!"

"Call 999," said Nick, and he ran into the alley.

Alison picked up her phone. Her hand was shaking as she dialled 9-9...

166

The blow came from behind. She slammed into the wall. The bricks scratched her face, and before she could work out what was happening, she was on the floor.

Alison was dazed more from the shock of the situation than the injury to her body. She gazed at the concrete ground and then felt a sudden pain in her right side. She had been kicked. Another kick to the torso winded her.

She heard Nick shout, but she couldn't place from where his voice came. A part of her brain told her that if another kick came it would all be over. Her ability to fight back had a use-by date. She pushed herself up, turned. The boot was coming down. She threw herself backwards, and the kick glanced off. Looking at the face of the attacker, she saw a man, tall, muscular, early forties. His face was calm.

She pushed herself onto her feet, took a crouched position, arms defending her body, feet ready to move. She felt a presence to her right, as did the attacker. He moved his body, no longer directing the attack towards her. Alison glanced to her right to see Nick bearing down on the attacker, and euphoria filled her. She was safe. But then she noticed something was wrong. The left side of Nick's shirt was covered in blood.

Nick took a swing at the assailant, but it was a swing that was slow and wild. The man brushed him away, and Nick almost collapsed with the push. He tried again, flailing with his arms. The man grabbed him and spun him around so that he was facing Alison. Nick looked at her, a hint of apology in his eyes as the man pulled a blade out of his pocket and

167

stabbed Nick in the stomach. He pulled the knife out and then sunk it in again and again, fast, like a piston.

Nick hit the ground, his body like a rag doll. The man smiled at Alison.

"It's over," he said.

He turned his head. At the end of the alley, another man had appeared. This man was more wiry and younger than her attacker.

"Just do it," said the wiry man, smiling coldly.

The muscular attacker moved towards her.

As the man came at her, the world in Alison's head slowed. She had been attacked before, but this time was different. She had learned. She had trained for this moment, endless hours at evening lessons invested, and this was where they would pay off.

The blade glistened in the man's right hand. She was crouched. He would try and pull her up. Slashing downwards would be difficult and messy. He didn't think he had anything to lose, so he would work to get her into position. Standing against the wall so he could stab into her abdomen. Damaging organs, less likely to strike an artery.

Two armed men, one unarmed nine-stone woman. Queensbury rules weren't going to cut it here. She reached in her pocket, found what she was looking for. The man was right on top of her now. She sprung upwards, her house keys protruding through her fingers, and punched as hard as she could, straight into the guy's balls. She felt the keys cut into her skin but obviously not as much as he did, a point evidenced by the scream of agony.

Alison's brain was still evaluating. Muscle memory kicking in. Step one over. Step two action, reaction. The man was going down. His head and hands would be coming down to his groin. The physics of biology. His right hand would be holding the knife. He would probably be in no position to use it, but this would all be for nothing if she impaled herself on the blade.

Her left hand came up, deflecting his arm. With her right hand she continued the upwards movement. Aimed her punch at the guy's open chin. Metal met skin. Metal won. The keys continued on their upwards trajectory until they hit bone. With her left hand, she grabbed his wrist, his hand still holding the knife. She dodged to the left to avoid his falling body. Her right hand joined her left, twisting, letting gravity do the work. As the man fell, his heavy muscular body worked against the position of his arm, which snapped. He screamed in pain again. Alison grabbed the knife from the man's now useless hand, and as he smashed into the ground, Alison was standing knife in hand.

The wiry man looked at her, aghast. Less than two seconds ago, it was all over. Now his colleague was on the floor screaming. He was having to quickly recalculate, and his brain wasn't dealing well with the task.

Alison's brain was coping far better at assessing. Running was an option; the muscular man had not anticipated her resistance. That would not be the situation with her next opponent.

If she did run, he might catch her. He might not start after her straight away, though, and if there were people on the street, she might be able to get to safety. But she was in heels; he was in flat shoes. Advantage for him. There was also Nick to consider. She was almost certain he was dead, but there was still a chance. If she left him, that chance would disappear.

Option two was to fight. Hand-to-hand combat. She had seen off the muscular guy easily enough, but that was defensive action against a person not expecting resistance. Her Krav Maga training had taught her well for such an occasion. Unfortunately that training had not been so concentrated on what to do on a one-on-one knife fight. The rule was fight back and get out. Back to square one on that front.

Alison needed a third option. She shouted at the top of her voice, "Fire!" The wiry man looked at her like she was a fool, but it was a hard truth of human nature that people would not run towards trouble. If people thought there was a chance of being stabbed, they stayed away. In a crowd, that reaction would be amplified. Basic group dynamics. A person in a crowd was freed from responsibility to act by those around. He would look to that crowd for information on how to react. Everyone waiting, each looking to the other for information. The result was inaction. It was that result that could lead to a woman being killed in a public place with no one lifting a finger to stop it. Alison knew that, and that is why she shouted

170

again, "Fire!" People would run to a fire. Maybe it was an inbuilt reflex to protect your own property. Maybe it was that no one ever got stabbed running towards a fire.

Alison readied herself for the attack. If he came at her it would require defensive action. He was a smaller man and so would be less likely to rely on his strength. He would come in slashing. His reach was longer than hers, so in a slashing fight, she would lose. If he did come at her, she would close the gap, take away the reach advantage, and look to disable him with a knee to the groin.

He was holding the blade in his left hand. A southpaw. Alison would be defending with her right arm. Right-arm deflection. Splayed fingers into his eyes. No one expected that. Chances? Fifty-fifty maybe. He had wounded Nick, so he had some skills. So did she.

She shouted "Fire!" again. Waited for him to make his move. He did. He ran. Sprinting away up the alley and not looking back. Alison took a breath. And then she looked over at Nick on the ground. It had been only half a minute since they were walking calmly to his car, but that now seemed like another lifetime. She ran over to him and looked down at his lifeless body. Blood had started to pool on the ground. She bent over him.

"Nick?"

But there was no movement. She reached for his neck, tried to find a pulse. Her fingers found skin. There was no movement beneath. No pulse. No heartbeat. He was dead.

And then with the adrenalin waning, the reality of what had happened hit. In a moment, Nick had been killed. A feeling of grief and horror swept over her. She screamed. Tears filled her eyes. The woman who had shown such soundness of mind only seconds before was gone, her mind now trying to make sense of the dead body in front of her.

"Are you okay?" said a voice in the alley. Alison looked to see two men walking towards her. She wanted to run. The older of the two men reached into his pocket and pulled something out. He showed it to Alison. Her mind ticked over, trying to make sense of the card.

"Police," said the man. Her mind shut down, emotions flooded her system - anger, fear, relief, grief, sadness, embarrassment.

"You're safe," said the older man, calm authority in his voice.

Alison just looked at him.

The younger policeman moved to Nick's body. He looked down, recognised the victim. "Jesus!"

"What is it?" asked the older policeman.

"It's Nick Drake."

Alison felt a strong desire to protect Nick. "Don't hurt him," she said, knowing as she said it that it was illogical. She knew he was dead. She had felt for a pulse. There wasn't one.

"It's okay," said the younger policeman. He reached for Nick's neck.

Alison felt hope. Maybe she had done it wrong. Maybe the adrenalin had reduced her ability to detect a faint beat. But then the policeman turned to his colleague and shook his head, and Alison knew that he was gone.

The policeman stood up and looked to the other body in the alleyway. Alison had almost forgotten about him. The sound from the alley came back to her. The man was screaming.

"What the hell happened?" asked the older man.

Alison willed her lips to move. She wanted to tell this man of the trap, of Nick, the hero, walking into danger to protect a stranger, and of the two men, one of which was on the floor. But her lips didn't move.

The younger policeman knelt down next to the muscular man.

"Holy...!"

"What is it?" asked the older man.

"He's got a bunch of keys stuck in his face."

"He killed Nick," said Alison.

The older policeman nodded towards the muscular man. "And what happened to him?"

"He underestimated me."

The older policeman looked around. The alley was empty. "We need to control the scene. I'll take the woman back to the station. You call it in."

The older policeman looked at her. "What's your name?" he asked.

Alison was silent for a moment and then said, "Alison."

"Well, Alison, we are going to get you out of here. Take you somewhere safe. Everything here will be looked after by Tom.

There's nothing to worry about now."

Alison heard the younger policeman talking. She turned to see him speaking into a handheld police radio.

"Alison, come with me," said the older policeman, holding out his hand.

"But Nick," she replied. "I need to stay here for Nick."

"He's gone, sweetheart. I'm sorry. But now we need to get you to safety."

Alison looked at his outstretched hand.

"Time to go," he said.

She found herself reaching out and grabbing his hand, like a dream. No, a nightmare. Her body was moving, her head trying to keep up.

He started leading her away. Moving down the end of the alley. Out onto the eerily silent main street.

The policeman led Alison over to his Volvo. He hit the fob on his keys, and the car bleeped. Moving Alison towards the rear door, he opened it and guided her into the seat, using his hand to protect her head.

Alison sat in the back, stared forward. The older policeman got in behind the wheel.

"What is your name?" asked Alison in an attempt to introduce a moment of normalcy on a very unnormal day.

"Jim Rawlstone."

Rawlstone turned the keys, and the car moved away.

SIXTEEN

"I can't believe what they're saying about him," said Sally.

They had been talking for over an hour, and most of the conversation had been about the biker. Spencer wondered what the woman facing him would think if she knew that he was doing his very best to kill the man about whom she was so concerned. Telling her that it was a choice, the biker's life for Spencer's, probably wouldn't have helped. Yet Spencer knew that those were the stakes now. The Emissary had erased all doubt of that. Of course, Spencer had always planned on killing the biker anyway, so the him-or-me argument wasn't strictly speaking logical, but where did logic fit within love?

"He's not a killer," continued Sally. "He wouldn't hurt a fly, and especially not Charlie. They were best friends."

Spencer was getting tired of hearing about the innocence of the man. So what if the biker hadn't killed yet? He was soon going to kill Spencer by the omission.

Spencer was on edge. He had hoped that their meeting would calm him, but just knowing what was going on a few miles away meant he couldn't truly be in the moment. He thought he had been nervous over the Trent murder, but it was nothing compared to how he now was feeling. That murder had involved a high level of preparation, and nothing had been left to chance. What's more, Spencer was protected if it had gone wrong. He had taken great pains to hide his true identity, but with Banner out of town, he had been forced to get more hands-on, put his face into the open more often. He knew the risks, but he had no choice.

Now he had to associate with people who knew, if not his name, at least his occupation. If they failed and were caught, it had the potential to end up back at his door.

"Nate loved Charlie. Nate just couldn't grow up. He kept remembering back to when he was travelling. Nate, Charlie, and Brian. He referred to them as the Three Amigos. The silly sod."

And suddenly Spencer refocussed on the conversation. There was something, maybe nothing, but still…

"There were three of them travelling? You mentioned a Chris?"

"Brian Knowles. He wasn't with them this time. He lives in Germany with his wife and child. Nate hadn't seen him in over a year. Brian was the grown-up."

"What was he doing in Germany?"

"He works in something to do with import or export. Big money, apparently."

Spencer's mind was working overtime. The big question had always been how the biker had re-entered the country. The Arabs had his passport - it was the one thing they had got right. Yet the biker had managed to smuggle himself into the UK even though there were warrants out for his arrest across every European border. Maybe all he needed was a friend in the right job?

Spencer's train of thought was interrupted by his mobile vibrating in his pocket. He reached into his jacket and with trembling fingers pulled out the phone. He looked at the screen, and his heart started beating faster and faster.

"I'm sorry. I have to take this," he croaked.

He hit the button and put the phone to his ear.

The tone of the voice on the other end told him what was coming even before the first sentence had formed. It was a fuck-up. Sally looked towards him and smiled. Spencer said "understood" and hung up.

The room closed in on him. The sound of the crowd became louder, almost deafening. His heart was beating so fast he seriously thought he might be having a heart attack. He was hot, so hot, he could feel beads of sweat trickling down his face. But she was in front of him, watching, and he couldn't react. He couldn't scream or cry or do any of the things that could make the feeling go away. He had to hide it. He was a spy, that was what he was trained for, pushing the fear away

177

so that it wouldn't show. Yet the woman in front of him was suddenly looking concerned.

"Are you all right? You've gone pale."

Spencer had to react, but his brain had frozen, and he couldn't for the life of him think what to say. Spencer needed to think, to take a moment, to weigh the options - but there wasn't time.

"My sister is dead," he spluttered.

Sally looked back, shocked, and then stood up from her stool. She took a step towards Spencer and threw her arms around him in a hug. He reciprocated, putting his arms around her. She felt soft. It was a softness that felt like home, a softness of safety. In that moment, no one could harm him. He moved his head to face her. And then without even realising it, his lips were on hers, where they remained for a fraction of a second before she pushed him away.

. . .

David had been on the move for what felt like a lifetime. His wet shoes had been rubbing against his soles, slowly removing the skin like vicious dermabrasion. Now every step was agony. But he knew he had to keep moving.

Stark, thin trees reached high into the sky and stretched on into the distance for as far as he could see. The scene was otherworldly, like a film location representing an endless struggle. David had been trudging through this same scene for hours. To try and distract himself from the pain, he had decided to treat the arduous endeavour as if he was an actor in a role. He was playing a man in a fight against futility, boldly walking forward when every molecule of his body was screaming at him to stop.

It wasn't his only technique for continuing on. He had taken to finding a spot on one of the trees in the distance, selecting one with some small deformity or deviation so as to be able to keep track of his target, and then he'd count the steps until he reached the mark on which he had been focussed. Each time, he convinced himself that once he got to that special tree, he would look out and see civilisation, and in doing so know that he had made it. He had lost count now of how many times that on reaching the target tree, he was met with an identical view of yet more trees. Yet each time he had repeated the process, and he was sure that the tree he was now heading towards would reveal the way out.

In many ways, the tree game, as David had decided to call it, was not that different from being an actor. When he had set out on his acting career, he had given himself ten auditions, after which he knew he would get the part that would change his life. Those first ten auditions had rendered nothing. David had considered giving up, but not for long. He knew he hadn't given himself enough of a chance. He decided that fifty was the new number. Fifty auditions came and went. There were a handful of paying gigs, but that big life-changing role remained elusive. But still it was not time to quit, and the number had been increased to one hundred, and then two hundred. In some way, he concluded, every failed audition was as painful as the footsteps he was taking now. And then David took another step on blistered feet and realised that was bullshit.

David had considered giving up acting many times, but in the last few weeks he had made the decision to quit. He had been kept afloat by the magazine, but with that going to the wall, it was time to grow up. But now, with the threat of death hanging over him, that had all changed. The whole shitty experience had given him a chance to examine his priorities. Whilst he had regrets, not one of them was linked to choosing to become an actor instead of an accountant. He had a dream, and God damn it, he was going to carry on. With that realisation, David reached the target tree. He was about to pick another tree as his target, but then he found a better destination, because through the trees, he could see a cottage.

· · ·

They had been driving for around ten minutes, and Alison spent the time reliving the attack, a memory that ended each time with the look on Nick's face when the knife entered his body. She tried to shut out the image, banish it, but like an angry squatter claiming rights, the shadow of violence wouldn't leave.

She tried to get her bearings. They were in an area of London with which she was unfamiliar. Large structures of glass and chrome had given way to small buildings of brick and rust. As the journey continued, those buildings became more and more sparse until they were replaced by the wasteland of deserted industry.

"Where are we going?" she asked.

"To the station."

"Which station?"

"Almost there," he said. "I need to check on something first."

The car moved past a high-wire fence that ran for several hundred metres in each direction, and in the middle, a huge steel gate stood open and waiting. The car slowed and turned into the opening. The wheels hit rougher ground, and the vibration and sound increased as the vehicle moved down the overgrown driveway towards a ramshackle factory.

"What's going on?" asked Alison, concern growing in her voice.

"Nothing to worry about."

"Why are we not going to the station?"

"We are. Just not yet."

The car moved past a rusting factory, which was clearly no longer in use, and manoeuvred onto a flat cemented area that ran for a hundred metres in each direction. At one time, it would have been a car park for workers, but now weeds had fought through, and the cement had ceded and cracked, creating a surface of murky grey and green.

Rawlstone stopped the car, pulled his phone from his pocket, and dialled a number.

"Why are we here?" asked Alison, growing impatient.

The policeman held his hand up in a gesture to wait. He smiled. "Just a moment."

He turned his attention back to the phone. Someone had answered.

"It's DI Rawlstone. There has been an incident. One policeman down. The attacker has been injured. PC Davis is making arrangements back at the scene."

The self-preservation element of Alison's brain kicked in. Things felt all kinds of wrong. She wanted to escape. If she was wrong, it would be embarrassing, but if she was right… She pulled the door release quietly, but the metal bar moved back without resistance. The door was centrally locked. "Shit!" Alison muttered under her breath.

No," replied Rawlstone in answer to some question that Alison couldn't hear. "Understood."

Rawlstone ended the call. He reached a hand into his pocket and swung his body round to face her. Arm outstretched, gun in hand.

Alison reacted instinctively, grabbed his wrist, and pushed his hand away to the right as he pulled the trigger. The windscreen behind her head exploded, and shards of glass sprayed her body. The noise was deafening, and a harsh ringing replaced all other sounds.

She held firmly to Rawlstone's wrist and kept pushing his

hand away from her head. He tried to reach over the headrest with his left hand to grab her collar. His fingers made contact, but he was too far away to get a proper grip. Alison bent her head down, put her teeth around his little finger, and bit down as hard as she could.

Rawlstone cried out in pain and pulled his hand back. Alison could taste his blood in her mouth. She pulled her feet up, planted them on the rear of the passenger seat, threw her head back, and pushed back for all she was worth. He was stronger, but she had physics on her side. Rawlstone was pulled into the seat.

The gun went off again, the bullet firing out of the shattered back window. It was so loud that Alison feared her ears might explode, but she kept pulling his arm. Moving her hand slightly, she positioned her thumb on top of Rawlstone's trigger finger, pressed down, and fired again. He fought to keep his finger from moving. She pressed again, but he twisted his arm, moving the trigger away from her thumb. Taking her left foot from the chair, she planted a heavy kick in his face. He cried out. With Rawlstone momentarily distracted, Alison was able to move her thumb back over his trigger finger. She pressed down.

Bang. Bang. Bang. Bang. Click. Empty.

The ringing in her ears muted all other sounds, creating in Alison's head a violent, silent movie of survival.

She kicked him again. Harder. He recoiled, holding his face. Alison planted both feet on the chair and kicked back,

183

pushing herself out through the shattered window. Fragments of glass pressed against her back as she wriggled through the gap. She placed her arms on the window frame and pushed herself out, part falling, part sliding down the car's boot.

Alison threw her hand back to prevent her head hitting the gravel-covered ground. She landed in a heap. Her ears ringing, pain wracking her body. She had to move. A fraction of a second, act or die. Get up! She pushed her hands down onto the gravel, forced herself onto her feet. She could see Rawlstone opening the driver's door, ready to follow if she ran. She needed more time. Running would be futile. He would catch her - his shoes were far more practical in a footrace.

Alison sprinted around to the driver's side door. Half open, Rawlstone already had a foot on the ground. Alison threw her body against the door, slamming it against his leg. He cried out in pain. She pulled the door open and then swung it back. Rawlstone tried to extract his leg but was too slow. The metal slammed into his shin. He screamed again.

Alison opened the door to swing again, but this time he got his leg inside, and the door slammed closed. Alison looked at him through the glass. They waited a moment, each trying to work out the next move. Rawlstone moved his hand up to the window, hit the catch, and locked the door. Alison watched as he leaned over to the glove compartment. Opening it, he pulled out a small box. It took her a fraction of a second to work out what the box was, but when she saw him tip bullets into his hand, she understood.

She looked on the back seat, to where the gun was laying. Rawlstone looked around for it, saw the direction of Alison's gaze and turned, seeing the gun. They both waited. Standoff. Alison weighed up the options. The door was locked. In order to get to it, she would have to break the glass. If she had a baseball bat, or even gloves, then maybe, but all she had was her bare hands, and that meant punching though the window. Even if that was possible it would probably mess her hand up enough to make it difficult to defend herself.

Rawlstone dove for the gun.

Alison ran.

She hoped she'd damaged his leg enough to slow him down, but she couldn't outrun a bullet. It would take a matter of seconds for him to reload. The wasteland ran for several hundred metres in every direction. If he was a good shot, she was dead.

The only other option was the factory. Alison sprinted towards it as fast as she could. She didn't look back. Just kept her legs pumping.

She ran towards the large doors. They were closed, but maybe she could force them open. If not, she would run around the side and try to find cover. But getting closer, Alison saw the door was held shut by a heavy padlock. No way through. So she kept running, straight past the door and around to the side of the building.

A series of bushes partially blocked the way. Alison didn't slow, barging through, branches scratching her arms. She was behind the factory and had cover, but that wouldn't be the case for long. She had to either hide or get out of range, but without knowing his location, it was difficult to know which was the better option. He could be just on the other side of the building. If that were the case, running would be fatal.

She looked ahead. No door, but plenty of broken windows. Next to one of the windows, a set of wooden pallets had been stacked carefully. The window above was gone, just an empty gap in the wall remained, with a staircase for the homeless looking for a roof for the night. Alison took the pallets at a run. They creaked under her feet. She reached the top, but the window was still above her. Alison jumped for the ledge, fought for purchase, strained, and pulled her body up and over.

She fell into the building, hitting a raised platform. She took a breath and tried to listen for Rawlstone's approach, but her ears were still ringing.

Dropping down from the platform to the level below, she looked around. It was dark, but the remaining light of the day crept through the windows, enough to see the room. A raised platform around the sides produced the feeling of being in a large shallow pool.

The building had long been abandoned. Hypodermic needles on the floor showed that the factory had taken on a new role. Alison scanned, looking to see if she was alone.

She moved across to the other raised platform and pulled herself up as silently as she was able. She ducked under the window, needing to know where he was. Peeking out of the window, she saw him, twenty metres away, limping and mad. She ducked back down.

Running was no longer an option. Her eyes scanned the building for a suitable hiding place. She crept towards the back of the "pool". The platform level was higher there, and Alison could see the remnants of rusted machinery and waste stretching beyond into darkness. Moving towards the back of the factory, past machinery that looked like presses, mechanical Goliaths that had been used before work was shipped off to China or replaced by automation, she found cover behind one of the machines.

She waited, her ears still ringing. Her eyes scoured the floor for anything she could use as a weapon. A handful of hypodermic needles lay along the ground. She could hope that he'd die from a particularly fast-acting strain of tetanus, but that was unlikely. The glossy pages of a magazine lay on the ground close by. Alison bent down to look and was met by the sight of a barely clothed eighteen-year-old on the cover. Maybe the internet had not killed off print pornography after all. At least, it seemed not, for those that also had a liking for hardcore intravenous drugs.

Alison bent down and picked up the magazine. She rolled it up, and then, reaching into her pocket, she found a spare hair band. She doubled up the band and rolled it down the magazine to hold it together. She would have preferred a crowbar, but beggars can't be choosers, and she knew the effect a rolled-up magazine could have if used correctly. And she was going to use it correctly.

Three hypodermic needles lay around her feet. She picked them up.

The main door rattled. He wouldn't get through that way unless he had the key to the lock. He would likely find the way in as she had.

Then, through the ringing, she heard the sound of scrambling by the window. Rawlstone was in the building. Alison tried to control her breathing. Those who panic die, those who think live, she reminded herself. Her training had served her well already in the last hour. One more victory was needed. She had to focus on the gun, work to reduce its hole-forming ability by keeping the loud, dangerous, bangy end away from her body. He was right-handed and would have an advantage if turning left. The natural swing of the body would turn the gun in a wider angle, providing the best kill shot. Where she was now meant he would have to wait until he could get his arm at the correct angle before he could fire. It would provide no more than a second, but Alison knew that could make all the difference.

She could hear his footsteps on the ground. He was in the pool. She heard him grunt as he pushed himself up onto the raised platform. He was twenty feet in front of her. She didn't look, didn't move. Surprise was her best weapon, and that meant using her damaged ears only. Anticipating his movements. Knowing her strategy. Being ready to adjust the strategy if needed. Keeping calm. Years of Monday nights in a leisure centre had been tested, and so far they had proven the best investment of her life. Keep calm. Be back there in the leisure centre. Smell the sweat, see the mats. Just another exercise.

First, she had to take the gun off the table. Breaking his arm would be the best option, but doing that without bringing the gun within the radius of her body would be difficult. Taking the gun was another option, but also problematic. She could break his wrist, but the wrist didn't have the same leverage options as the arm. He was undoubtedly stronger than her. If she got into a one-on-one wrestling match, the odds would be in his favour. No, she would have to be strategic. She would have to fight dirty, just as she had been taught.

The ringing in her ears had been replaced by the sound of her own heartbeat. She found herself holding her breath.

Relax. Being oxygen deprived isn't going to help. She knew now that a fight was inevitable. And this wouldn't be like being in the leisure centre. There would be no laughter after a practiced move. She would not be going for a quick drink with this person. There would be no conversation as to how their respective bruises were going to show next day. Alison was about to fight for her life for the second time in an hour. She had to win. It wasn't just her life that was at stake. They were trying to get to her because she was close to finding David. Two lives to one. Alison had been searching for an identity for most of her life. Most of the roles she had tried on hadn't

189

fitted. But Alison knew who she was now, and in a matter of seconds so would Rawlstone. Alison was a badass.

She waited. Listened for his footsteps. Closer and closer. She pushed the rolled-up magazine into the neckline of her blouse. It was her secondary weapon. It would be used, but she had a plan for a first assault, and pornography didn't figure. The primary assault would involve the hypodermics, the ones that were now jutting between her knuckled fist like ultra-fine claws. She could hear him breathing. He was close enough to touch.

Remain calm. Wait for the moment.

She saw the pistol first. Inches from her face. The end of his outstretched arm, his finger on the trigger, ready to fire. But she remained still and waited. Not yet.

He took another step, bringing his elbow into view. Now!

She stepped forward and swung her right arm round in a wide arc. Her clawed fist flew towards his eyes. She hooked her left arm around his gun arm and pulled him close, trapping his arm against the metal beam. Her right hand continued its journey through the air. The needles moving faster and faster as the energy of swing increased its momentum, that momentum retarded only by the bridge of his nose. One of the needles bent and fell to the floor, but one stuck in his forehead. The final needle found a home in his open eyeball.

Rawlstone screamed and tried to pull away, but Alison held him firm. Her right hand, now free of the needles, moved back, and in a fluid motion she grabbed the rolled-up magazine and pulled it from her blouse. There was no wide swing this time, just a short stabbing motion towards his throat. The magazine made contact, and the fifty glossy pages compacted and stayed firm as they impacted his larynx.

Rawlstone dropped the gun. Alison knew there was no need for her to pick it up. The fight was over. Rawlstone fought for a breath that would never come. His windpipe had been shattered. Alison had often wondered whether pornography led to violence against women. In this case it was the other way around.

Rawlstone fell back and collapsed to the ground, drowning on dry land. Alison had studied first aid. A tracheotomy would save his life. She had never done one, and she wasn't going to start now. He had been involved in the murder of Nick and possibly even David. She had cared for both of these men, and this man dying in front of her had played a part in taking them away from her.

She stepped up to him, looked at his eyes, and saw the panic, the fear, the realisation that life had come to an end. Maybe in that moment he was questioning what lay beyond. If that was the case, he was likely praying the answer was nothing. He looked at her, begging her to do something. She did.

She watched him die.

SEVENTEEN

David felt like crying. He had run on pained feet towards the cottage, but when he reached the front gate, hope had disappeared. The crumbling brickwork and broken windows indicated that the cottage had not been used for a long time, a realisation rendered concrete when he banged at the front door and received no response. The place was deserted. He used a rock to break the lock on the door, and the rotten wood crumbled with the first impact.

He kicked open the door to reveal an empty and somewhat out-of-time cottage. The place still had a fully fitted kitchen and looked like it had been cleared in a hurry, and badly.

David was starving, so he headed towards the kitchen. It was a long shot, and when he pulled open the cupboard, he was hit by the smell of damp. His heart leapt when he saw a line of cans, all without labels. He guessed that the labels now made up the mush on the bottom of the cabinet. It didn't bode well. He pulled an unidentifiable can from the cupboard and started opening drawers to find something with which to open it. He didn't need to look far, for in the first cupboard were a handful of knives and forks, and more importantly a tin opener. There was also a newspaper, but David was way too hungry to give that any attention.

The tin opener was of the old style, which involved piercing the can. As he punched through the tin, he was hit by a pungent smell. He almost vomited on the spot, but his hunger drove him on, and he cut and levered the implement around the corners and pulled the top open. The contents were black and putrid. If he was to guess, he would say that they probably used to be peaches, but it was clear they were now inedible.

David slumped back to the floor. If this was a test of character, he was failing.

Then he remembered the newspaper. Maybe that could give him some clue as to where he was. He pulled himself up yet again and recovered the newspaper from the drawer. It was faded, but unlike the cupboard, the drawer had withheld the damp. He looked at the title. It wasn't in English. At a guess, he would say it was Cyrillic. More worrying was the date on the paper. He couldn't read the month, but he could see that the day was the 26th, and the year was 1986.

He collapsed back to the floor, lay down on the black carpet, and closed his eyes.

. . .

Alison looked down at the dead body that lay at her feet. It had been a strange couple of days, all in all. People spent their lives wondering what they would do in a range of impossible scenarios. Would you kill a man if it saved a hundred? What about a child? What if you had to do it with your bare hands? Were you still prepared to kill? Most people never had to answer those questions. They could accept that if it came down to it, they would take the best wrong answer.

Well, Alison had just had that question posed to her in real life, and the answer was clear. She could have saved him, but she didn't want to. That was not the answer she would have picked on a hypothetical test, but then again, her situation had not been hypothetical. Alison had become a killer by assault and omission, and if she were to tell the truth, she was fine with it. Now she had to work out what to do with the body. It was just the first of a seemingly impossible set of tasks - but first things first.

She bent down and reached into Rawlstone's pocket. She felt around, found what she was looking for. It had the feel of a wallet. She pulled out a folded-over piece of leather, a little larger than a travel card. She opened up the flap and looked inside. It was the warrant card that Rawlstone had shown her in the alley. There were only two possibilities: the card was fake or Rawlstone was a serving policeman. The card certainly seemed real. The name and photo matched. It could be a good forgery, but more likely it was the real deal. If it was real, then she had just killed a policeman.

She looked at the pistol on the floor. She was being hunted, and they wanted her dead. A gun could equalise the odds. Yet so far Alison had been successful because she was well trained and had simply put that training into action. She had never held a real gun, let alone fired one. She had to imagine that those hunting her were trained. If they knew their way around a handgun, she would be back to a disadvantage. What was worse was the gun might give her a misplaced sense of confidence.

More importantly, though, Alison needed the gun to remain on the floor. She needed it to be found next to the policeman with his prints still on it.

She had to accept that this was a policeman, and that meant that her opposition was powerful. How powerful was unclear. How many of them was not known. Yet they had carried out an impossible murder. They had kidnapped her best friend and had killed Nick. The odds were stacked against her, and Alison knew she had to level the playing field.

When they had killed Colin Trent, however they had killed him, they had set up a narrative that would force those who might ask questions to look the other way. They had created the story of a man killed by his own self pleasure, and they had spun it to the point that no one would ever ask the right question. It was little more than PR. Now it was Alison's turn to grasp the narrative - and the narrative started with a dead policeman. That dead policeman would be found with a gun lying next to him. That gun would have his fingerprints on the grip. The gun wouldn't have been registered to Rawlstone as a policeman. Nothing about him shouted armed unit, and even if he were, there was no way he would commit a murder with a gun that could be traced back. A dead policeman and an illegal gun with fingerprints. A bent cop.

Alison's narrative relied on the fact that her enemy was limited to a small number of bad apples in the police and a handful of others who would kill for money. If Manson was right and the state was involved, then no narrative was going to save her. But Alison had enough faith in human nature to risk her life that most of the police were closer to the likes of Nick than Rawlstone.

She knew that the building had been used by drug users. They were not here now but could be at any second. Leaving the body and hoping it would be found was not an option. She would have to point the finger. A phone call to 999 would do the trick, but she couldn't use her phone. A pay phone would be ideal, but outside of Central London, they were few and far between.

Alison had to think. And she had to fight back. She had to solve an impossible murder. She had to find her friend. She had to take down those who were trying to kill her and those who had killed Nick. She had to do it with no money and no phone and without returning to her home and her bed. She had to do it without going to the police. Then she just had to work out what the fuck was going on. Easy.

Alison wiped the warrant card on her jeans. Her fingerprints were not on file, as she had never even had a driving conviction before today. But now she was a murderer, and although it was in self-defence, there was no need to incriminate herself any more than needed. She threw the porno mag to the corner. The glossy pages of naked women fluttered to the ground like a teenage boy's dream of snow. Alison never shared the view of some of her readers that the police lacked imagination, but she was pretty sure their imaginations wouldn't extend to this particular murder weapon.

She looked around for the dropped syringe, wiped it against her jeans. Ordinarily she would not be minded to rub a heroin user's hypodermic needle against her clothes, but this was far from an ordinary circumstance, and looking down it was clear that her clothing had survived less well than she had.

Moving over to the dead body, she knelt down by Rawlstone's head and did her best to wipe any prints from the hypodermic that had punctured his eyeball. The sight made her sick to her stomach, but she wiped until the barrel was clean. In the centre of his head, a needle stood alone. The body of the syringe had fallen away. Alison looked around the corpse but couldn't see the broken hypodermic. It may have fallen under his body or under one of the old machines. No time to search further. She had work to do. If the police did search for prints, they were going to find hundreds, probably all of them drug

197

users, many with criminal records. The police station would be full by morning. She wouldn't be on their list. They would investigate but draw a blank. As they did so, the question of why a policeman was found dead with an illegal gun would grow.

Alison dropped back to the lower floor and headed for the window she had entered through. Although she would have liked to leave no trace of herself, there was no time to clean everything. If they looked hard enough, they would be able to tell she'd been there. She couldn't worry about that now. She had to get far enough away. Others might be after her. They might have known Rawlstone's location. He had phoned it in.

The phone! If she couldn't use her own phone, maybe she could use his.

Alison climbed back up to the window and through to the wooden crates. She walked quickly down and back towards the car.

The car sat abandoned, the front door still open. Alison had not found any keys in Rawlstone's pockets, and she hoped they were in the car.

On the front passenger seat lay Rawlstone's mobile. The keys were still in the ignition. The phone had probably fallen out of his pocket in the struggle. The keys were a sign of a man in a hurry to chase down prey. More importantly, the scene showed that Rawlstone hadn't intended to hang around. He had underestimated her, and it had killed him.

Alison didn't look good. Her jeans and blouse were ripped

and dirty, and her hair was a mess. In the past, this would have simply been a cosmetic problem. Now her state held more significance. She needed to disappear, to head for the shadows, to fight them in the dark. It was so much more difficult to hide in the shadows when you looked like you'd been literally dragged through a bush.

She looked around the car for her handbag. There'd been no time to collect it when she was fleeing. She found it underneath the driver's seat and realised she must have kicked it down there in the struggle. Reaching around the seat, she pulled out the bag. She was going to need money, but there was less than twenty pounds in her purse. There was a debit and credit card, though. Maybe she could withdraw some money with those? Alison needed to think, but she would do that away from here. She sat on the driver's seat, closed the door, and started the engine. She had already committed murder, an additional bit of car theft wasn't likely to make the situation worse.

Alison swung the Volvo round in a wide arc, and the wheels crunched against the gravel. She took a final look at the building and headed for the gate, hoping never to see the place again. She would find her bearings, phone the police, and report a dead body. She would keep moving.

But first she was going to need some assistance.

EIGHTEEN

Alison used Rawlstone's phone to call the police after only ten minutes on the road. She made it to something close to civilisation, where she ran into a late-night newsagent and purchased a sandwich, a pen, and a pad of paper. The sandwich would have been disappointing under any other circumstances, but at that moment it was the best meal she'd ever tasted.

She ate in the parked car and once finished turned her attention to Rawlstone's mobile. It was cheap but practical, not a smartphone, something that would have been fashionable ten years ago but now could be picked up as a pay-as-you-go for £10. She pulled up the call log. The phone was empty of detail, no contacts, no messages. There was only one number logged. The phone call that Rawlstone had made before he pulled out the gun. Alison wrote down the number. She wasn't going to call now. That would tip off whoever was on the other end that Rawlstone was dead. She wanted her enemy to think that the threat had been neutralised.

When she had phoned 999, she had told them only that there was a body and the location. She had thought about mentioning that it was a policeman but decided against it. They would come to their own conclusions soon enough.

Alison needed assistance. It was clear that she and Nick had been set up. Mr Brown had led them to that pub and had cancelled on them. He knew. Mr Brown worked for the government, so was the state trying to kill her? Alison couldn't believe that was the case. She didn't think that way. She needed to find a man who did.

. . .

The cottage was dark. Mattie shone the flashlight attached to his rifle around the living room. He scanned the room, finger on the trigger.

He heard a sound behind him and spun, his body reacting, his rifle moving to acquire a target, ready to do his duty.

Banner brushed Mattie's rifle away.

"Stop fucking around," said Banner.

He looked at Mattie's gun, reached forward, and flicked the lever on the side.

"Safety on! Orders are to capture. Plus, if you shoot me by accident, I will be extremely fucked off."

Banner swept past him, his semi-automatic slung across his shoulders. Mattie suddenly felt like a naughty schoolboy who had been given a dressing down by the headmaster. It was completely unfair. He knew what he was doing. This job was his destiny, after all.

The cottage stank. The smell of damp was the dominant note, but against that there was something else, something rank. Mattie followed his nose into the kitchen. He walked over to the sink and looking down he saw a can of black gunge.

"Okay, he's not here," shouted Banner from the kitchen. "Take a break."

Mattie dropped his rifle to his side. He was sure this had been the place. The front door had been smashed open, and now there was this can. The fugitive had been here - he could feel it.

Mattie walked out of the cottage, past the broken door, and breathed in the night air. He wished he smoked. This was a smoking moment, that was for sure. Mattie had tried smoking a number of times, but it had always left him feeling sick. He had tried it first when he was nine due to the loving actions of his father. The Bastard had lit up the stick and forced him to breathe in the horrid air. Mattie had thrown up before he was halfway through, and the Bastard and Deeko had found that very funny.

They didn't stop there, though. His father had punched him on the arm hard and told him it was against the law to waste a cigarette. Even at nine, Mattie knew that was bullshit. His father threatened to punch Mattie again unless he finished, so he put the white stick to his mouth and inhaled again. He vomited once more and would have done again but for the fact his stomach was empty. Ever since, on the numerous times he had tried to develop the habit, he couldn't - the taste smelt too much like sick.

Mattie's lack of smoking ability had been a major obstacle on his path to the dark side. Those three inches of rolled paper had been the entrance to the club of the loner, the maverick, the rebel. That had been where the hard men had always resided at school. In those hidden-away places, those who rejected life's rules had met with others who shared their mindset. Mattie should have been a member of those gangs. But he didn't smoke - couldn't smoke - and that had excluded him from where he belonged. It put him away from those boys. Worse, it made him stand apart and made him a target. Mattie had learned early that you needed to find a group. Without it, you were prey. He knew that was where the others would be now. Those three inches of paper were excluding him once more.

Mattie switched off his torch and stood in the darkness. He waited for his eyes to compensate. A half-moon provided some light, but Mattie could make out only the barest of details in the landscape, mostly a shit tonne of boring trees. If the captive had been in the house, where would he have run? Mattie wondered what he would do if he were being chased. What if he were the prey?

. . .

Alison drove up the ramp of the multi-storey car park, all the way to the uncovered top level. It was late, and the small number of cars parked had decreased with each successive storey.

She pulled the Volvo into one of the bays, leaving the car in the centre of the white lines. She may be a killer, but she knew that was no reason to drop her standards, for once basic parking manners went out the window, society was really in the shitter. She looked at herself in the mirror. A few days ago, life had been so different. She had worried that she was becoming boring - that wasn't so much of a worry now.

Alison reached into her bag and pulled out a small packet of paper handkerchiefs. Removing one from the packet, she used it to wipe the steering wheel. She followed with the gear lever, seat belt buckle, and door handle. She closed her eyes, tried to remember every action since she got back to the car. She hadn't touched the radio, but she had switched on the headlights - she wiped the switch. Had she touched the window? No, she didn't think so. She wiped anyway. Clean enough. She hoped.

Covering her fingers with the hanky, she pulled the lever on the door and stepped out. She had considered holding on to the car. Part of her just wanted to get on the motorway and drive somewhere far away. But she had a job to do. Her friend was in danger, and she wasn't going to find him by running away. But saving David was now only part of it. They had messed with her life, tried to kill her, and they had killed Nick. Nick had been a good man, and that good man was now dead. Those fuckers were going to pay.

Not wanting to be enclosed, she didn't take the lift, instead opting for the stairs. She wanted to be able to run.

She walked down ten flights and came out onto the street. It was 11 p.m., and the pubs were kicking out. The road was still busy, as Alison knew it would be. She had picked it for that very purpose. Those who had attacked her had used isolation as a weapon. Alison's plan was to stay in the light. If they were going to attack her, they would have to do it with the world watching.

. . .

It was a shambles. They had failed to kill the girl. Worse, they had been so sloppy as to be injured and killed themselves. So much for being the best of the best.

The backup team had been even more incompetent than the rest of the jokers. The junior partner at least had the sense to ferry the injured moron back to the hotel, rather than let him be taken to the hospital. Spencer had given the kill order, and that should have been it. But no. He thought it was bad when he received the phone call in the bar. That phone call took him over the edge and led him to make a fool of himself. But now Rawlstone had been found dead, with an illegal gun next to him. Who the hell was this woman, the Terminator?

Two policemen had been killed in a single night, and questions were being asked. Spencer hated questions.

In the room next to him, he could hear muted screams. With the majority of his people still away looking for the escaped prisoner, the hotel was close to empty. Spencer had been more than disappointed to see the reaction of the few men that remained upon seeing their injured colleague. He was sure that some of them were going to faint. Looking on the bright side, at least they wouldn't have to break into the woman's house next time, as they had her keys. The fact that they were stuck in the jaw of a trained killer was a minor inconvenience.

Spencer opened the door. The so-called killer in question lay on the bed. A doctor who would ask no questions had been summoned and had bandaged his face. Spencer had tried getting some sense out of the injured man, notably how the fuck he'd managed to let a five-foot-six woman insert her keys into his face but hadn't got much of a response. The killer had tried his best to speak - he had that much decency, at least - but all that came out was a string of nonsense, interspersed with screams of pain. It was pointless talking to him. With the bandages on his face, it was even difficult to know if he looked ashamed. Well, he bloody well should.

Spencer was losing. He knew it, and the people in the base could feel it. This was where good management came in, rallying the troops, making difficulties into opportunities. But the truth was, his heart wasn't in it. The fear of death at the hands of the Emissary now felt less important than the pain of humiliation he was feeling. What the hell was he thinking? Of course she wasn't going to kiss him back. He had needed to be patient. With the knowledge he had about the woman, he could have worn her down over time. He had gone from stranger to hugging buddy in less than forty-eight hours. The bedroom was in sight, but he had blown it. Now the dream was over.

On the bed, the killer screamed again. Spencer felt like smothering him with a pillow. Pushing down until the life ebbed out of him. That's what a Roman general would have done if a soldier had shown his level of incompetence.

Spencer had to get a grip. After all, it was simply a matter of tracking down three separate fugitives, then killing them in a way that wouldn't raise any questions. What could be simpler? Spencer knew the answer was everything.

. . .

Alison stopped short of her destination. Looking left and right, she scanned for suspicious-looking people. If they were there, they were not obvious, and the street seemed to be populated only by a handful going home for the night.

She had no reason to suspect that she was being watched. It was unlikely they would have found the car yet, and she was sure that no one had seen her at the factory. The police had to have found the body now, but even if they had, there was no way of tracking it back to her - at least no way of doing so quickly. Or so she hoped.

She was about to retrace her steps, and that gave her cause for concern. It was late, and she hoped the person she was looking for was in and would get to the door. She had always been taught though to prepare for the worst, and that was why she opened up Rawlstone's phone again, flicked though the log, and found the phone's own number. She pulled the pad and pen out of her bag and in large print wrote the number onto the page.

As Alison walked to her destination, she kept alert, constantly checking behind her to make sure she wasn't being followed. Within ten minutes, she was at Manson's shop. It was in darkness. She took a final look around and then pressed the buzzer. She waited for a response, for the speaker to crackle and be filled by Manson's voice, but it never came. Instead she heard a buzzing. She looked around, trying to place the location. It seemed to be coming from a speaker placed by the side of the LED sign. A sign that was now illuminated by a singular word -

"Run!"

Alison turned and saw three men walking quickly towards her location. They all looked to be in their sixties and would be with her in seconds. She had to move. But first she pulled the page back on the pad and pointed the page where she had scribbled the mobile number at the camera. She hoped that

Manson was still watching.

A man was approaching to her right, another to her left. In front of her, the third man was walking quickly over the common. Alison ran. The common gave her the best option. She saw the men to her right and left start to run. She was so fixated on them that she didn't notice the car that was speeding down the road. Brakes screeched. Alison kept running. It stopped inches away from her leg, and as she ran she could hear the annoyed driver screaming through the open car window. She kept going. Running straight towards the man on the common. She would try and get past him. If she could outrun them, that would be best. If not, she would have to fight. But there were three of them; the odds of being successful were remote.

Always play the odds.

The man in front stood still. Bouncing on his toes like a veteran tennis player readying to take a serve. It was British Bulldog. Alison had played it at school and always lost. Now, losing wasn't an option. Closer and closer. She could hear the men behind panting. Heavy footfalls.

Alison dodged left. The man moved to catch her, but then she veered off right. She dummied, and it almost worked. He was slow to check back, and she was inches from being free and clear. But the man managed to grasp her collar with his fingertips. She felt the resistance against her neck. Fight or flight? A decision made in a fraction of a second. She planted her feet and spun. Taking a step forward on her left leg so as to

209

be face-to-face with the man, she drove her right knee forward, hard, into the man's groin. He went down. They always did.

The chasers were about five metres away. They had fallen behind. She was younger and faster, and they knew it. Alison turned and ran further into the dark common.

She kept her legs pumping, her speed fast and regular. The panting behind her faded. They were falling further and further behind. She didn't look back. If they had a gun, there was nothing she could do now. A handful of people were around. She hoped that that was enough to prevent them opening fire.

No gunshot came. Alison kept running. Her phone rang, but she kept running. It nagged away at her, but she knew that she couldn't risk answering until she was clear and safe.

She reached the middle of the common. The phone was still ringing. She risked turning round. Her pursuers were gone. She stopped, reached into her bag, pulled out the phone, answered it with an out-of-breath "Hello?"

"Did you get clear?" It was Manson.

"I think so," said Alison, the adrenaline causing her voice to quiver.

"Don't think, know. Keep moving."

Alison started walking, quickly. She took deep breaths. Tried to get her heartbeat back to normal.

"What the hell are you into?"

"I don't know. They tried to kill me. They killed my friend."

"They have been following you for days. I spotted them as soon as you left. They tried to break into my place, and I decided that was the time for me to leave. I packed a few toys."

"What do I do?" asked Alison, trying to keep the desperation from her voice.

"Do you know who they are?"

"I know one was MI5. I met him. He called himself Mr Brown."

"You have to disappear."

"I need to find David." Alison looked behind once more.

"And you won't be able to if you are dead. They have shown their hand. The die has been cast. They can't let you live."

"But where do I go?"

"Forget everything you're used to. If MI5 are after you, then it has been government sanctioned. They will be everywhere you know. Your friends and family are off the board. You go to them, you die."

"I need to get money."

"Not on your cards, you don't. If it's the state, then they have access to your account. They will be waiting for you to take out money. The moment it happens, they will swoop."

"I'll draw out money and then move on."

"Not fast enough. You need to work on the basis that your money is toxic."

"Where can I stay?"

"You need to improvise. You can't sleep rough. They will be on the lookout for that. A small hotel is the best bet. One that takes cash and doesn't ask questions."

"I don't have cash."

"Steal it."

The implication hit Alison hard. She stopped walking.

"I'm not a thief!" she blurted.

"You have to lose the woman you were two days ago. You have to kill her, or they will. Lie, cheat, steal. Do whatever it takes to stay ahead of them."

Alison glanced behind again, and then resumed walking quickly.

"And how do I help David?"

"Make the world ask the questions that your enemy doesn't want to answer."

"The website?"

"Is down. I tried it this morning. They will have your internet history. They will be watching every site you ever visited. You're going to have to be smart."

Alison was getting close to the road. She stopped. Looked for cars. "They could be anywhere."

"Understanding that will keep you alive. One last thing. You need to throw away this phone."

"It's not mine," she said.

"I know. If it was yours, we wouldn't be speaking. Where did you get it?"

"I ran into trouble. The man that caused the trouble didn't need it after we met."

"Jesus!"

"As it turns out, I am far more frightening than they imagined. Actually, I'm more frightening than I imagined."

212

"I don't want to know what happened. And you don't want to tell me. But they will find out that you have his phone, and then they will have something that they can track. Ditch the phone."

"How will I contact you with no phone?" said Alison, her obvious panic showing once more.

"You need something untraceable."

"Have you got a number I can call you on?"

"I don't have a phone."

"You're speaking to me now," she cried.

"From a call box."

"You're kidding."

"I never kid," he said.

"So you're not contactable?"

"Get a phone. Get me your number. I will phone you."

"I can't come to your place again. How am I going to get the message to you?"

"Be smart. Think it through. Hide in the shadows at all times. Whisper messages so only those who know how to listen will hear."

And then the phone went dead. Alison looked at it for a moment. And then the phone started ringing again.

She hit the green button.

There was silence on the other end.

"Hello?" said Alison.

"To whom am I speaking?" said a voice Alison recognised from somewhere.

"Who is this?" replied Alison, the fear rising in the pit of her stomach.

"I asked first." Alison's mind spun, trying to place the voice.

"Mr Brown?"

"Give up, Alison. There is nowhere to run."

Alison could feel her heartbeat. It didn't help that she thought Brown may be right. She took a breath, gathering herself.

"You bastard!"

"I have been called worse things in my life."

"You are not going to get away with this."

She stood still, then turned in a circle, scanning her surroundings, looking for an attack she thought was inevitable.

"Yes, I am. You are outnumbered. They will find you within the day. Hand yourself in now. We can negotiate."

"Like you negotiated with Nick."

"I would have stopped them if I could. This is bigger than you can imagine. Look at who your opponents are. Do you think that the forces that control these people would ever let you succeed? They have too much in the game."

"Who are you working for?" she demanded.

"You know the answer to that, Alison. You pay my wages, after all."

He was trying to keep her talking. She wanted the answers, but knew that every second she was on the line was a second she could be tracked. She hung up, and then, still walking quickly, threw the phone as far as she could.

She was on her own and needed to think. But first she needed to be away from here. She knew where she would go. Somewhere she would never be tracked. Somewhere she was never allowed to go.

To see a man she had never wanted to see again.

NINETEEN

David was lying on the ground when he saw the hunter turn off the torch. He had been lucky - if that was the right word. He had been asleep, dreaming of being warm and safe. Alison was in the dream - they were laughing, working at the magazine, him in front of the camera, her behind. It was a scene that had happened many times in real life, a scene he now realised he had taken for granted. But then in the dream, a bird had flown in through the window.

At first they had laughed, but as the bird circled and flapped, the mood changed. The flapping wings got louder and louder, and the panicked creature tried to fly out of the closed window. The creature smashed into the pane. Its body fell to the ground where it lay quivering, close to death. David looked at Alison. He didn't want to leave her. She took his hand. And then she screamed three words: "They are coming!"

David had awoken in a sweat. Maybe it was just a bad dream, but every cell in his body told him he had to flee. And so, with no logical reason, he had opened the door and run as fast as his injured feet would carry him into the darkness. He had been hobbling less than a minute when he saw their torches. He had thrown himself down on the ground behind a tree, and that was where he still lay, staring at the man, standing in the darkness in front of the cottage that moments earlier had been his shelter.

And then David saw that faint figure move. He switched his torch back on, illuminating the ground in front of him. David watched as the lit patch of ground moved slowly towards him.

. . .

What would Mattie do if he were hunted? If he were panicking? If he had no time to think and only just enough time to act? The cottage had a back door, but that had been closed and bolted from the inside when they entered.

How does the prey react when startled? It runs, follows a straight line, the path of least resistance. Mattie would have hoped that if he were the prey he would have been smarter, changed route, found cover. But he had experience enough to know that panicking people are rarely smart.

Mattie took a step forward, switched on his torch, and looked at the ground. A fleeing fox does not think about hiding his trail from the dogs. He relies on speed alone.

Maybe there would be tracks. The ground showed nothing. It was firm and not willing to collapse underfoot to give up tell-tale footprints. Maybe there would be other clues, items dropped, foliage moved. Mattie always used to like Westerns. He remembered those Native American trackers. He was a tracker now.

He continued forward, swinging his torch across the ground in a wide arc, methodically examining the ground, looking for the trail. Mattie was looking for something hidden, and if there was one person on earth who was designed for that, it was him. Mattie had experience.

. . .

David pressed his body to the ground. The figure with the torch had kept walking. The man had taken five minutes to halve the distance between David and the cottage. It was clear that he hadn't seen him. He was searching for something. If David didn't know better, he would have thought the guy had lost his keys.

David's heart was beating through his chest. It felt so loud that he feared the man might hear him. He tried to work out his options. The beam of light would hit him in a matter of minutes. When that happened, the only option would be to give himself up or to fight. The figure was far enough away that David couldn't see if he had a gun, but the guys back at the house certainly did. He had to assume the man was

218

armed, which altered the chances of winning a fight from extremely unlikely to really, really, extremely impossible. But running was even less likely to be successful. He had always been quick on his feet. At school he had won the hundred metres on sports day. He probably still had some of that speed from his youth, but even excluding the fact that his feet were in the state that they were, the chances of him outsprinting a bullet seemed slim.

David looked around for a weapon. He saw a fist-sized rock on the ground. It was close to him but still out of reach. He dreaded moving. Logic told him that as long as he kept close to the ground the pursuer would not be able to see him, but in the battle for his mind, logic was coming a distant second to fear. And fear was telling him to keep still and hope it all went away. He fought his base instincts. Pushed his body sideways with his hands. Keeping his body tight against the ground, he inched towards the rock. It took him less than ten seconds to reach and grasp it in his hand, but in his head, it seemed like a lifetime. The figure continued walking towards his location. Sweeping the beam of light. Getting ever closer. Close enough now that David could see the outline of a rifle in his hands.

He was going to have to fight. An untrained man with a rock against a trained killer with a gun. It didn't seem fair, really. Maybe if he stood up and explained he had never been in a fight in his life the pursuer might take pity on him. Because that was the way the world worked after all, wasn't it?

The beam was getting nearer and nearer. David held the

rock in his hand. He lay there, silently holding his breath, praying that the man would head off in another direction. But he didn't. He just kept heading straight towards him. Less than ten metres away now. Maybe five more steps until the light reached him. He had to act. His heart beating, he weighed the rock in his sweaty palm. He would leap at him. Strike him on the head with the rock, summoning every ounce of strength he had. But David knew that this was unlikely to work. He knew the man would gun him down before he had even got off the ground. David was about to die.

And then a faraway shout echoed through the trees. The man stopped, turned. Maybe this was David's chance? He willed himself to stand, to leap, to strike. But nothing happened. He just lay there.

And then the man started walking away. David's prayers had been answered.

. . .

Mattie heard the cry from behind him. He turned and saw a figure by the house waving a torch. It was the prearranged signal that it was time to pull out. Mattie wanted to stay longer. He felt he was close yet had seen nothing to evidence the fact. Even though Mattie wanted to stay, he feared being left behind, and the attitude of Banner earlier suggested that this fear was not unfounded. Mattie turned and reluctantly walked back to the house.

He would never know how close he was.

. . .

David lay on the ground for twenty minutes. Part of him was convinced that it was a con and that they were just waiting for him to stand and give up his position. Yet no further sound was heard, and he was getting cold.

He stood and began to slowly walk back to the cottage. His eyes searched for oncoming killer bastards, but there were none. They had searched the cottage and not found him.

Just as he was about to push open the door, he saw a small red light flashing on the floor. He looked closer. It was a red LED light attached to a box, a box that had not been there an hour before, a box that would prevent him getting a comfortable night's sleep. Because David knew he couldn't go in. The romanticism of sleeping under the stars was over. He wanted a warm bed and boredom.

TWENTY

Alison looked up at the house. This was a low point. She hated being dependent on someone else, and she especially hated having to be dependent on him. She contented herself with the fact that in any other circumstances, this would be the last place she would be. She was here because she knew there would be no trace of this relationship, if for no other reason that she never wanted anyone to know about it.

Alison felt the guilt all over again. She had never planned to be the other woman, but that was what she had become. It had been a short affair, a meaningless series of encounters with her boss. The only problem was that it hadn't been meaningless - at least not for her. She would never stand in the way of a husband and wife for something meaningless. She had loved him.

She watched and waited, hoping that he hadn't changed his

habits. The hall light flicked on. When she knew him, he was a workaholic who got up at the crack of dawn. Those were the times he used to phone her. She would usually still be asleep. They would have whispered phone conversations back then. That time seemed another life away now.

Alison waited for ten minutes and then walked across the street towards the house. She had never been there before but remembered the address from his HR forms. Not that she was a stalker or anything. She'd just wanted to know more about him. At least, that was the lie she told herself.

Now that she was here, it wasn't what she had expected. Jim had always given the impression of a man in love with the city, yet this place was about as suburban as it came. The house was large and semi-detached. The garden was neat and precise, flowerbeds and manicured grass. Alison walked along the path that led to the front door.

As she approached, the light in the front room switched on, illuminating the garden. Alison froze on the spot. Looking through the window, she could see a living room, TV, and sofa. And then she saw him again. He had a phone to his ear. Nothing had changed.

Alison watched Jim sit down on the sofa. He hadn't seen her. He looked the same as he had three years earlier. Back when they had been lovers.

Alison stood, watching a scene from her previous life. It would have been her he was phoning then. Was this where he had spoken to her? She wondered who was on the other end of the line, wondered if it was another impressionable colleague. One more drink after everyone had left the pub. A quiet kiss, and then it would get sordid.

She crept up to the window, raised her hand to tap the glass, and then froze. She couldn't do it. There had to be another way. Someone else. Something less complex. But then the matter was rendered moot because Jim looked up towards the window and nearly jumped out of his skin when he saw an old lover on the other side of the glass, her hand seemingly raised in a black power salute.

They remained fixed in position, staring at each other until Jim made his apologies on the phone and hung up. He stood and walked towards the window. Alison wished she looked better, more composed and slightly less mad. Unfortunately, the activities over the last hours had moved cosmetic issues towards the bottom of her agenda. But now she knew. She saw it in his eyes. He thought she had bought a ticket on the crazy train. And she was going to have to tell him a story that wasn't going to make that impression any less questionable.

He shrugged his shoulders at her. What do you want?

She pointed to the front door.

He paused, thinking it through. Alison knew he would be fearing for his dirty secret. Hell, the way she looked, he was probably fearing for his safety. With his wife upstairs, it would be a risk inviting her into the house. Alison thought he would try to manage his way through the situation. That was his style. A quiet word would stop her from making a scene in front of the wife and neighbours. But what if he didn't? She might be waiting there for hours, just staring through the window, like a dog banished from the house. She could make a scene, but would that be any more likely to gain her the support that she needed right now? Would it heck! Alison was gambling. The ball was spinning around the table, black or red. She waited for the ball to drop.

Jim nodded towards the door. Stage one completed. Now the tricky part.

Alison waited for what seemed like minutes. Where was he? And then the garage door next to her began to open. The automatic mechanism wheezed and grinded. To Alison it sounded like the loudest noise in the world.

She walked towards the garage, the door now half open with only Jim's legs visible. It continued in its upwards sweep until he was fully visible. She wanted to run and hug him. She needed that support. But that was then, and this was now.

"What are you doing here?" he whispered.

She walked forward.

"I'm sorry. I had nowhere else to go."

When she was inside the garage he hit the button and the door began to wind down. "You can't come here. Jenny is upstairs."

"I am not here to make a scene. I am not trying to get you back. I'm sorry. I'm in big trouble, Jim. I need your help, and then I'll go, and you'll never see me again."

He cringed slightly. "Soft voices."

225

"Sorry."

"What's happened?"

And so Alison took him through the events of the last few days. The impossible murder, the missing friend, the attack.

"You killed a man with a porn magazine?" asked Jim.

"Not the most important part," said Alison, trying to keep as calm as possible.

Jim looked at her, trying to work out if she was for real. She had been logical in her narration - or so she thought, but it was hard to tell someone you were in the middle of a government-backed conspiracy without sounding a little mad.

"What do you need?" asked Jim.

"Money. I need to book into a hotel and clean myself up. I can't use my cards; they'll track it and show up at my location."

"You honestly think that the government is out to get you?"

"I know it sounds mad. If someone had approached me with this story, I would be looking at them the same way you are. But you know me, Jim. Probably better than anyone. Better than I want you to. Have I ever been one to exaggerate or live in a fantasy?"

"How much money do you need?"

"Enough to check into a hotel without raising questions. I also need some clothes. I'll pay you back. I just need to find somewhere safe for a few days. Somewhere they can't find me."

"If you feel you're in danger, go to the police."

She looked at him incredulously. "Have you been listening? I can't. They are the police."

"So you thought."

"I saw their warrant badges. They were real. It was an assassination. We were set up by MI5. We were told where to meet the spook. He manoeuvred us into position. And yes, I know this sounds crazy, but it's real. I am not making it up. My life is in danger, and I need help."

"And I'm the only one you can turn to?" he asked, unable to hide the disbelief in his voice.

"You are the only one they can't find out about. I kept it secret, Jim. It shouldn't have happened. I shouldn't have let it happen. But now you're all that I have."

He looked at her. Weighing up the options. Working out if he could trust her. "I can give you money."

"Thank you. I will pay you back. You have my word." She paused. "I don't suppose you have a spare laptop, do you?"

. . .

David awoke to find himself staring at the cottage. It took him a minute to work out where he was and why he was lying on the cold ground. When he eventually remembered, he wished he could close his eyes and go back to sleep.

He had been dreaming of Chris again. The dreams would always come when he most needed them, as if Chris was watching over and protecting him. David had never been a religious man; he didn't believe in Heaven or Hell and so logically he knew that Chris wasn't really overseeing his life.

227

Yet right at this moment, ideological belief systems seemed like a secondary consideration. The dream had given him strength. Chris's life may have been ended by a cruel and unstoppable antagonistic force, but David was damn sure his wasn't going to fall to these sad sack bullies.

He pushed his body up with his hands. It was time to press on. They had passed him in the night, and so, in theory at least, they were in front of him. But turning back wasn't an option. For all he knew, there was another wave of hunters behind him and to his right and left. He had come this far, and he was going to continue on the same course.

. . .

Jim dropped Alison off at Oxford Street. She had told him everything she could back in his garage, and now that that was out the way, there seemed little to discuss. The journey was largely silent, as though every word had been expressed back when they were together and neither had any further words to give.

Alison had carried the laptop in a carrier bag she had collected from the garage. She had asked to be dropped at Oxford Street for a number of reasons. She did have shopping to do, but mostly she just wanted to be surrounded by people. She had always felt able to melt into the crowd and become anonymous. She had only ever been attacked when the crowd was gone and shadows dominated.

Alison had a plan. It was a plan that was largely dependent on being able to work out what David had seen. She had to get the message out, and if the website was not an option, she was going to have to go old school.

. . .

David had been walking for hours. His feet were still painful, but the overnight rest had at least allowed his shoes to dry. He had continued to aim for selected trees and lost count of the times he reached the target and reset the game. As the day progressed, the trees changed, and the bare foliage that had been the view for the past day gave way to shorter trees with green leaves.

And then, halfway between the last target tree and the next, David walked out of the woods onto a wide tarmacked road. Beyond the road, the forest continued, and a few metres farther was the tree for which he had been heading. The road had been cut into the forest and sat lower than the ground on either side, rendering it invisible until he was right beside it.

David turned his head to the right and saw the road stretching off into the distance. He did a 180 and looked in the opposite direction. One hundred metres away there was a large hut, and from what he could see, it appeared occupied. Outside the hut, on either side of the road, two large poles were planted in the ground. One pole was painted red and black, the other yellow and blue.

It was the closest David had been to civilisation in days, and he picked up his pace as he strode forwards. The pain in his foot faded and his energy increased. He had raised his hopes at the cottage, and the disappointment had almost defeated him, but this felt different. In the hut, he could see movement. People.

David was safe.

TWENTY ONE

His heart had sunk when he reached the hut and was met with people carrying guns. For a second, he'd thought he had walked into a trap, and then he noticed that those with the guns also had uniforms, something that had been missing from the men who had held him prisoner.

The two guards had taken a hard look at David, although as much as anything, that was probably due to the way he looked. His clothes were caked in mud, and his face and hair were a mess. David explained he was British, and the guard had spoken to him in broken English. Once David had explained the situation as well as he could, the guards pointed him to the bathroom, and he was able to have the best shower of his life. The shower was powerful and warm, and the dirt fell from his skin. David hoped that, like the dirt, his awful experience was now behind him.

When he turned off the shower, he heard voices in the room beyond. There seemed to be more than two. Maybe the guards had called the authorities or the British Embassy?

David looked for his clothes, but on seeing the muddy material on the floor, it was clear that the term no longer applied to them. There was no use putting them on, as it would have instantly rendered the shower futile. The guards had yet to bring him a change of clothes as they had suggested they would. He looked around the shower room. There was a locker in the corner, and David pulled the door open in the hopes of finding a dressing gown. What he saw instead were four yellow plastic one-piece suits hanging on the rail. They looked like clothes used by Scenes of Crime officers, either that or hazmat suits. It was far from the soft dressing gown that he was hoping for, but he pulled one from the peg and quickly put it on.

The voices outside the room continued. David moved to the door as quietly as possible and slid the bolt back. He opened it a crack and looked through. The guards were chatting to two men. The older man was talking in a language David couldn't understand, but it was the man standing behind him that caught David's attention - mostly because it was the scar-faced guard he had pegged as the leader back at the house.

With his heart beating quickly, David closed the door and clicked the bolt back across to lock it. He looked around the room for a way out. Other than the door, there was a small clouded window along the top wall. It would be tight, but he knew it was his only option. The window was too high up to reach. Looking around, he saw a metal bin in the corner. He grabbed it and ran over to the window. Flipping the bin over, he stepped onto it and reached up to the clasp. It was stiff but finally moved on the third tug. Each tug moved the bin a little, and David worried the resulting squeak would be heard behind the door. He pushed open the window and jumped for all he was worth, throwing his arms over the ledge he pulled himself up and through.

David fell headfirst eight feet but managed to turn and take the impact on his back. He hit the ground hard and air was pushed from his lungs, momentarily rendering him unable to move. He turned his head as he tried to get a breath. The hut was based on wooden legs, and he could see underneath to where a dozen booted men were standing.

He had to move, and so pushed himself up. The forest was only ten metres away. But running would bring him out into the open and make him visible to the men on the other side of the building. It really didn't help that he was dressed in fluorescent yellow.

From the room above, he could hear banging on the door. Once they realised he was not answering, it would be broken down and then it would only take them a fraction of a second to work out where he was. He dipped his head and looked again under the hut. Many of the feet were climbing the staircase into the building. David hoped that the rest of them were directing their attention to the noise being made inside.

He had only one chance. Keeping as low as he could, he sprinted towards the tree line. As he did, he heard a loud crash behind him, and he knew they had broken down the bathroom door.

He made the tree line and kept running, his now bare feet seemingly impervious to pain, rendered numb by sheer terror.

. . .

Alison checked herself into a hotel at noon. She had taken the Victoria line to King's Cross and, thinking that it would be a good place for hotels, had left the station and headed down the main street. If she didn't know where she was going, how could those hunting her find her?

She had found a hotel that in Goldilocks terms was neither too big nor too small. She checked in under a false name, and when asked by the receptionist about the reason for her stay, she said she was there on business. She hoped that the trouser suit she'd bought earlier gave weight to that impression. The clothes that had been on her back for the past twenty-four hours had been bundled up and stuffed in a recycling bin. Whoever ended up with them might be given to wonder what had happened to the original owner, but they were unlikely to come up with the correct answer.

She entered the lift to go to room 428, hitting the button for the fourth floor and then holding the lift door open for an older man who smiled at her for her kindness. He also alighted on the fourth floor but walked off down the corridor in the other direction, so Alison didn't pay him any further attention.

In her room, she collapsed onto the bed. She hadn't planned to lie there more than a few minutes, but exhaustion took hold and sleep overwhelmed her.

When she woke, the clock on the TV read 5.15 p.m. She had been dreaming of David. She saw him lying in a box on a table. It was the famous cutting-the-woman-in-half routine - or in this case, David. But as the female magician brought down the saw to his body, she morphed into the fat, smiling figure of Mr Brown. As the saw cut into David's skin, Alison awoke. The images of the dream made her feel nauseous, and she cursed herself for losing so much time. She had to watch the video again. The answer had to be there.

She remembered the nightmare. The image of the magician's blade ripping into David's flesh made Alison reflect. Perhaps it was a particular skill set that David had that enabled him to solve the mystery? If that was the case, then all she needed to do was think like David. She knew in this situation he would ask how a magician would deliver the impossible. Alison jumped off the bed, opened up the laptop, and started the video at frame one, watching with the eyes of a magician.

. . .

David trudged on. More trees. More foliage. More pain. And now he knew there was no one he could trust. The forces hunting him had power, that was clear. Enough power to reach across Europe and manipulate those who were supposed to be a line of defence.

As he walked on, the trees disappeared, and he found himself on the bank of a river. On the water, two large rusted boats were listing, like gravestones on water. The boats looked like trawlers. The scene was surreal, but David was getting used to that. The last two days had been like being thrown into a world after a zombie apocalypse, with lives discarded in a need to run.

He turned and followed the river. After two hundred painful steps, he saw something in the distance and the surrealism of the day increased.

It was a Ferris wheel.

David walked along the deserted street. Blocks of flats ran along either side of the road, but in each, the windows were missing and the buildings were crumbling.

Maybe there had been a zombie apocalypse after all.

TWENTY TWO

Mattie climbed the eight flights of concrete stairs. The place was creepy, like a home to a lost civilisation. He reached the top floor, where a fire door blocked the way. Mattie pressed down on the bar and pushed. The door gave, but only fractionally at first. With another hard push, the door opened enough to allow him to squeeze through onto the roof. He looked down to see dust, rubble, and bricks, pushed aside by the door like angel wings in snow.

Mattie walked forward, his footsteps held in ash on the floor like an astronaut's on the moon landing - the one that had never happened. Mattie made his way over to the edge, taking cautious footsteps, concerned that the floor beneath him would collapse.

When he reached the edge, he looked over and surveyed the ghost city in front of him. They had all been warned that the abandoned city of Pripyat was now a tourist trap, although it wasn't Disneyland. But from the rooftop, Mattie could see no one save a hobbling man dressed in a yellow onesie, who seemed to be doing his best to resemble a crippled six-foot condom.

. . .

David heard movement, and when he turned, he saw five armed men sprinting towards him. His heart went into overdrive. He looked for escape, but there was none, and with his feet in the shape they were, he wasn't going to be able to outrun them.

To his side, the door to the nearest building was hanging open. David ran as fast as he could at the door, pushed through, and hit the stairs running. Taking them two at a time, he ignored the pain and exhaustion. He got to the top floor, which opened to the remnants of a large derelict office. He could hear the footsteps close behind. David was trapped. He ran into the office, looked at the window, desperate for some way out, even if it meant jumping. But when he got to the window he saw the street, at the end of which appeared to be a tour party. It took a fraction of a second to comprehend what he was seeing, but when he did, he took a large breath of air, ready to scream. But before he could let it out, he was tackled to the floor by two of the younger men. They held him down, and the largest covered David's mouth with his hand.

It was over.

TWENTY THREE

Spencer had returned to Thames House. He was tired, but he couldn't pretend to be off sick any longer without questions being asked by either of his employers. Eddington had given him the smiling third degree about how ill he had actually been. If only he knew what Spencer was really up to. Ever since Eddington had been promoted, he had treated Spencer like a lower employee. Eddington was a weasel, and Spencer could buy and sell him ten times over.

Spencer had received the coded text saying that a phone message was incoming and walked out of Thames House and onto Lambeth Bridge to take the call.

As he looked down onto the Thames, he dialled the number with a sense of dread. The way Spencer's luck was going, he wasn't expecting good news.

. . .

All through his life, Mattie had not made a fuss. He had kept his head down and made himself invisible. It was a trained reflex, which came from the environment in which he was dragged up. Anyone else would have wanted to be invisible too. What with the Bastard and Deeko just looking for an excuse to use their fists, anyone in their right mind would be quiet. Well, things had changed. Mattie had spoken up, and in doing so he had caused World War III. All he had done was raise his grievances.

It happened when everyone was in the plane coming home. Oh, they were all good friends now, the old commies and the young mercenaries were besties, and they were all gunning for him. Mattie had snapped. He had cried foul that the mercenaries had taken his money and he wasn't being paid. A smack was always likely, but it never happened - at least not to him. The commies had kicked off first. They were pissed off that they hadn't got a cut of the money. It was the bloody cheek of it that pissed Mattie off - although not as pissed off as the mercs had been. They said they had suckered Mattie into the deal and that the commies shouldn't be rewarded for the work that the mercs had done. They actually used the terms "suckered" and had done so while he was there.

What happened next was as unexpected as it was amusing. At least if your life savings had been stolen from you. The commies took umbrage, and so did the mercs. The speed with which punches were thrown was surprising, but that's what happened when you hung around with vicious scum. It was war. Mercs versus commies. Mattie's money would have been on the mercs all the way, but the result was far closer than he would have expected. The commies may have been as old as Christ, but they knew how to fight dirty. It had stopped being about the money very quickly. There had been tensions since day one. That became obvious with every kick to the head and punch to the balls. Luckily, all of the weapons had been locked away, otherwise it would have been a bloodbath. Mattie turned invisible again. Bones were broken and teeth were lost, and Mattie sat and watched, an island of calm in a sea of chaos.

It ended in less than three minutes, but the damage done was spectacular. It was without a doubt the most severe case of air rage the world had ever known. And then Banner had received a phone call. He had moved away from the commies, and it was clear that he didn't want those he still considered his enemy overhearing the conversation. The plane was large, but if Banner wanted a private chat, it meant that he had to come down the other end of the plane to where Mattie was sitting.

Mattie could tell from the way Banner was speaking that it was Fat Twat on the other end of the line. It was the only time Banner was ever full-out polite - at least unless he wanted something. Mattie listened in on the conversation as best he could. It sounded like Banner was being asked to go on a private job. He heard Banner say "I can finish her," and Mattie knew that there was some killing to be done. Banner looked over to Campbell, who was crouched over on the other side of the plane, holding what appeared to be a broken arm.

"No, we will leave him out of this. I can do it alone." Banner hung up the phone. He seemed to be in no hurry to head back to the other side of the plane.

Mattie spent the entire plane ride wishing he had never signed on. It was as though him becoming a killer was just not meant to be. But Mattie's mum had always said that things that were worthwhile were always difficult. She said that God had made it that way to get rid of all the people who didn't want it enough.

Mattie knew that God didn't exist, but the fact that he remembered this message did smack of some divine power showing him the way. He had lost almost all his money, but there was still five thousand pounds remaining. Mattie had never been in a casino but knew this was how it would feel due to the brilliant films he had seen. It was stick-or-twist time. Mattie thought of his mother. She had always told him to chase his dreams.

He knew what he needed to do.

...

Spencer looked across the Thames, wanting to cry out in victory. He didn't mind saying he had been nervous. A few hours earlier, he had been after three people. Two of those knew a secret that could unravel all of his hard work. The other person was just a nuisance. A large nuisance, to be sure, a nuisance that had managed to kill one of his best men and badly injure another but still just a nuisance. But now everything had come together.

They had followed the lead Spencer had obtained from Sally and found the biker. He had run, but the skills Spencer had employed his men for had suddenly proved valuable. They had found him again, less than a mile away. The biker had been discovered, and in a location that Spencer could utilise. It was a location that held fond memories for Spencer, as if fate itself had destined it be the location for his final victory.

He had originally planned to move the biker back to the hotel, but it was now safer to leave him where he was, as there was less chance of him being seen by prying eyes. He had been told that the stadium was secure, and a couple of calls to check this fact had confirmed this to be the case. Spencer's men were already on site, and they had locked down the new prisoner. This time they wouldn't have to worry about the prisoner outsmarting them. There would be no tricks. Spencer had given orders that two armed men should watch him at all times.

Where the first phone call had been about the biker, the call that followed less than two minutes later had been about the woman. They had found her. She wasn't dealt with yet, and it was true that the woman who had killed Rawlstone should be treated with respect, but then again, Rawlstone had been a corrupt drunk. This time Spencer was going to get his best man on the case.

The woman had killed Rawlstone with no planning but would undoubtedly have left a trail that could be traced back to her. Nick had proved problematic and hard to cover up. But now with two dead policemen, it wouldn't take too much effort to link them. The world hated coincidences. Evidence could be arranged, and Spencer had people in place who could put the evidence where it would do the most good. They probably had enough to do the job already, but if needed, they had access to her home, a place that would be covered in DNA. It was all about creating a story the world could get behind. The easy answer was always the most believable. Sure, she could make a nuisance of herself at trial, but Spencer would never let it get that far. Alison Aimes, who would be shown to be a murderer of two men, was going to commit suicide. That was a story people could buy.

Spencer the professional was back. He was thinking like a champion again. The master tactician had won. Eddington could be as arrogant as he wanted. Spencer would allow him that because Eddington was just a bulk standard civil servant, whereas Spencer was a god.

. . .

David had been in a stage fight on a number of occasions, yet he now knew that his performances had been fake. He had seen true violence in that plane. He had presumed that the people who had captured him were all one well-executed team. The truth had been revealed only a few minutes after takeoff. David couldn't work out how many factions there were or how they were divided. It was either British v Eastern European or young versus really, really old. David wasn't yet ready to accept death, but if it were to be his time, he really wished it not to be at the hands of those Muppets.

TWENTY FOUR

It took her two hours, but at a little past 7.30 p.m., she saw it. Alison knew how Colin Trent had been murdered. Now she just needed to get the message out. Or did she? She had purchased a handful of stick drives, along with stamps and envelopes. Her intention had been to record the little she had discovered and post the recordings to those who could spread the message. But with the knowledge of what was hidden in the video, Alison knew she had a bargaining chip, albeit a bargaining chip that would cease to exist the moment the information was made public. That didn't mean that the threat of the information going public needed to be removed, though.

Alison spent the next few hours compiling the information to the stick drives and putting them into envelopes.

She would phone herself at home, where she knew they

would be listening. Alison was going to give them a deal - David's life for their dirty little secret. The manila envelopes and their contents were her collateral.

But by midnight, exhaustion was once again descending. She would get up at first light and find a phone away from her safe location. From there she would put her offer to them and wait for a response. For the first time in days, Alison felt in control. And with this feeling of control, she lay down on the bed and turned off the light.

. . .

In the building opposite, two mercenaries watched the light in Room 428 go out. Mattie felt excitement in the pit of his stomach. Banner had said they would give it an hour before going in, but Mattie wanted to start right now. Patience had never been one of his strong points.

. . .

Spencer knew Sally was visiting her parents and would not return home until the next day. He had heard all the phone calls to arrange it. Her mother sounded like her. Of course, the reality was that if Sally was home, she would be somewhat freaked out to find Spencer standing in her living room. But he was on the verge of victory, and he wanted to share it with her.

The lock on the door had not been a problem. He had been a desk jockey for the past few years, but that didn't mean he had no skills. There had been no house alarm, as he knew there wouldn't be - it had been noted in the report when his team had put in the taps. Spencer was not a man to take chances when caution could be applied.

The flat was smaller than he imagined. The décor was simple, but some touches made it unique. The place was hers in the same way that her voice was hers. They just matched. It was perfect, like she was.

Spencer moved over to the bedroom door. The very thought that he was about to enter the place he had dreamed of made his heart beat faster. He placed his hand on the door lever, pushed down, and opened the door. The scent in the room was intoxicating. On the bed, there were more pillows than could ever be useful. It was the sort of frippery that he would have found annoying in anyone else, yet for her it seemed right. Along the walls, pictures of friends and family had been arranged into a mural. The room had the same feel as the rest of the flat - simple and classy.

There was no time to waste. He was here for a reason. He'd wanted to be closer to her, but after what had happened he knew this was as intimate as they would ever be. This wasn't a burglary; it was an act of love. With gloved fingers, he pulled out his mobile phone. The latex gloves were thin enough so as not to restrict the movement of his fingers, but they were irritating. Not in terms of his fingers but in terms of his soul.

He was in paradise and unable to fully experience it because of the powdered rubber. It was like fucking with a condom, adequate but undoubtedly missing something.

He put the phone back into his pocket and peeled off the gloves. They were unnecessary. He was being too cautious and in doing so robbing himself of the experience. Now the air of the magical place touched his hands. He pulled the phone back out of his pocket, and with it he took photos of every inch of the flat, the position of every drawer and the placement of every obstacle. Fingerprints would not be a problem because she would never know he had been here.

TWENTY FIVE

Even with the payment received, Banner did not seem pleased to have Mattie by his side, but at this point Mattie didn't really give a crap what pleased Banner. Mattie was there not just because of the money but because he was the only one who could be there. Campbell's arm had indeed been broken. The fact that the arm in question had been broken by a seventy-three-year-old Romanian made Mattie's heart sing.

Now everyone was back in the hotel healing, and whilst the physical injuries could be fixed easily enough, Mattie was sure that the emotional ones would never heal. The party was over. The fact that Mattie had in some respects caused the flare-up surprisingly didn't bother him. They were all sulking now. The commies didn't want to help out Banner because they were still pissed off that - in their warped heads, at least - he had stolen from them. Even the mercs had shown little interest in heading over for the kill. Mostly, Mattie surmised, because they had no faith that the commies wouldn't immediately shop them for murder. Mattie had no such qualms. He had nothing to lose.

And now he was with Banner, another man who had stolen from him. Mattie held no grudge. He was on the verge of losing his murder virginity.

Mattie waited at the rear door of the hotel. The stench from the bins was overpowering. He wished he had been the one to go in and book a room rather than Banner, but he had to admit Banner looked more like a businessman than he did. Mattie's stomach was doing strange things. He felt sick, whether it was due to the excitement or the bins, he wasn't sure.

Mattie heard a lever being pushed, and the door bolt moved. The door opened. Banner was waiting there and waved him in silently. Mattie was on the hunt. The feeling of nausea would subside soon. It was definitely the bins.

. . .

Spencer looked through every drawer, and yet he had found nothing to bring her closer to him. Maybe he shouldn't have come.

She was a neat freak, that was clear. All of her underwear had been neatly folded. He liked that about her. Yet he would have loved to find a diary or maybe a special toy of hers. To touch something that had been inside her would have been

252

like entering her by proxy. But there was nothing. Spencer felt alone.

There was one final place to look. He had seen it the moment he entered the room, but back then it had seemed disrespectful. Yet he knew it was inevitable. Although he had convinced himself that this was an act of love, he knew deep down it was about desire, and while love had boundaries, desire did not. Desire made men fools, prepared to sacrifice everything to scratch an itch. Spencer knew that was what had happened to him. She had cast a spell on him. A spell he needed to break.

And so he reached down and lifted the top off the laundry basket. He breathed in deeply, desperate to catch her scent in his nostrils. The basket was half full, a two-foot-tall column of divine material. On top of the pile, a white bedsheet. She had lain on that bedsheet. He reached his hands into the basket and slowly lifted the sheet as if it was more special than the Golden Fleece. He looked at the soft white material and then buried his face in it and breathed deeply.

. . .

Mattie watched as Banner picked the lock. The original plan had involved cloning an entry card. That would have been difficult, so it had been a relief when Banner had received an actual key upon his late-night check in. He had told Mattie he was an expert locksmith, but Mattie had begun to believe anything the lying shit said was a fabrication. Yet when they got outside Room 428, Banner had pulled out a small leather case from his pocket, inside of which was a series of thin metal tools. He had been at the lock for less than twenty seconds when the door clicked open, which was just enough time for Mattie to fit the nightscope over his head.

This was it. No going back. Both he and Banner had guns, but the plan was not to use them. That was okay as far as Mattie was concerned. He had held a gun when they were after the captive, and whilst Mattie had always dreamed of that moment, once the initial thrill had worn off, the reality had been strangely disappointing. He had found that the gun didn't fit. Even though his hand was the right size and his finger could easily press down on the trigger, the gun had never felt part of his body in the way he always thought it would.

Banner slowly pressed open the door. Inside, it was dark. They pulled down their nightscopes. Mattie had also dreamed of using scopes like this - like they always did in the films. He wanted to be like a Navy SEAL or an SAS soldier. But when Mattie pulled down the goggles, all he saw was a world of green that looked bleak and hostile. His heart was pounding. He felt sick to his stomach. The bins must have had more of an effect on him than he'd thought. Somebody really ought to do something about those bins.

Mattie wanted to remain still until the nausea passed, but Banner kept moving forward through the door, and Mattie knew he would have to follow. With the goggles on, Mattie could see that in Banner's hand was a cloth. The cloth appeared green, but then again so did everything else.

. . .

Spencer removed the sheet on the bed and replaced it with the one taken from the laundry basket. The duvet cover had likewise been changed. Finally, Spencer removed the pillows from the cases and replaced them with the ones from the basket. Now the bed was covered with material that had touched her skin and hair. Then he made a phone call.

As he sat waiting, he tried to convince himself that it had been a spur-of-the-moment decision. Yet he knew that was a lie. It had taken research and money to do what he was planning, but he had no choice. He was lost, completely besotted with a woman who would never be his. Deep down he knew that even if they did get together, it would be the beginning of the end. At this moment, she was perfect.

But perfection never lasted. Perfection offended the laws of nature. It is an unrealistic state. He had been in love before. That had seemed like perfection at the start. A woman had wanted to be with him. Perfection? At the time it had been a miracle, but before too long her mask had started to slip. She was not perfect after all. She was vicious and spiteful. Part of him was glad when she left. It taught him a lesson. Sally was only perfect from a distance. In the way that from a distance the stains and marks on a statue were not visible, so it was here. He wanted to keep her perfect but knew she was like a drug. She was intoxicating, and it was driving him to distraction. He needed to purge his system. That was why he was there, to connect with her for a moment in order to release himself from her. He was on the verge of victory, and she no longer fitted in his life.

And then the doorbell rang.

TWENTY SIX

Mattie crept forward. He could see the woman on the bed through the green mist of the goggles and could tell she was asleep. She had no idea what was about to happen. Mattie really wanted to throw up, but he kept it together. Banner was in front of him, a green mass of muscle and heft about to throw his body down on top of a fragile woman.

. . .

David was in darkness. They had placed a hood over his head the moment the plane had landed. He was forced forward, shuffling on still painful feet by two goons, one on each side, who held him upright with their arms locked under his armpits.

He had been listening for clues to his location. He had heard of blind people who developed their skills of hearing and touch once they lost their sight. David had only been blind for an hour or so, but he was hoping that he was a fast learner. The fact that they had dragged him from the plane handcuffed and blindfolded meant that it wasn't a runway at one of the large airports. A private or military airfield would be the most likely option. Either case confirmed that the people holding him had serious resources.

The obvious contender for the prize of Chief Evil Dickhead was the government. Who else could have that much money and influence? Yet if the government's hands were on this, the makeup of those who had captured, lost, and then recaptured him didn't fit his usual image of state actors. A few days ago, it would have been different. The three guys at the house could easily have been British forces. Since then, though, he had seen some of the others on the team and, well, they were old.

It wasn't just that they were old, clearly many of them were not British. He had heard two of them speaking a language he recognised as German, but another conversation had taken place in a tongue he couldn't specify, other than it sounded Eastern European.

The ground under his feet was rough, like a badly maintained path. He could faintly hear traffic. Civilisation was close, but he still knew he was farther away from freedom than when he was out in the middle of nowhere. He was a city boy, but now the city sounded foreign and dangerous.

He had been listening since the airport. The drive had

started quietly, a few cars on the road, probably countryside, but as they moved on, the traffic noise had increased. The car had finally stopped, and he had been dragged out. As he was carried forwards, he wondered if this would be the last place he would ever visit. Would he even be given a chance to see where he was going to die?

David tried to remember everything he could, every feeling, every noise. If by some miracle he was to escape, he wanted to bring the police back straight here. But he knew it was likely that escape was not going to happen. He'd had his chance, and it didn't work out. Life rarely gave you more than one chance. Death took a less strict approach. It didn't need to worry - Death always won out in the end. David now knew that it was going to win far faster than he had ever thought, but then again maybe it always did.

He heard doors slam and then the footsteps began to echo. It was a large space, hard walls, no furniture to absorb the sound waves. The ground under his feet was solid, probably concrete. His foot hit an uneven piece of ground, and he stumbled forwards. The arms under his pulled him upright and kept him moving. He counted the steps, he got to forty-nine before they stopped. He heard the rattling of keys, a key being turned in a lock, a door opening. The hands tightened on his arms, and he was thrown forwards. His feet gave way, and he fell. He automatically tried to bring his hands up to protect his head, but they were secured in front of him. He slammed into the floor. The weight of his body fell on his restrained hands. It was painful, but at least it reduced the impact on his head as it hit the hard ground.

The door slammed closed, and the key turned in the lock.

David listened. He heard breathing. There was someone else in the room. He prayed it was not who he thought it was.

"Hello?" he said.

No response.

"Alison?"

No response.

He tried to move his arms to take off his hood, but before he could do so, he felt the hood being lifted.

It was dark, but enough light filtered through the door to let him know that it wasn't Alison. The person in front of him was far bigger and significantly more male. David's eyes tried to adjust, and he was able to pick out the man's shaggy beard before he spoke.

"Hello?" said David.

"Better get comfortable," said the man. "We may be here a while."

"Who are you?" asked David.

"Name's Nate."

"Why are you here, Nate?"

Nate smiled sadly. "It's a very long story."

"I don't think I'm going anywhere," replied David, moving himself into a sitting position. He pushed himself backwards so he could lean against the wall and settled in for the promised long story.

· · ·

Alison awoke when she felt the hands around her body. A belt was pushed over her neck and tightened, and the leather bit down into her skin. She struggled, her mind trying to piece together what was happening. Alison felt her body being pressed down onto the bed. Something was on top of her. Her chest was being crushed. She was unable to breath. She tried to scream, but no noise came.

There was only enough light in the room to see an outline of the person above her - if it was a person. There was something strange where the head should be, as if she were being strangled by a cyborg. She could see another cyborg beside the bed. The belt seemed to get tighter and tighter. Her chest moved up and down rapidly as her lungs pleaded for air. She tried to swing a punch, but the creature on top of her pinned her arms with its legs. She tried to kick out, but the sheets above her legs restricted movement. She was being smothered and choked, and there was nothing she could do about it.

And then she saw the figure next to the bed reach for the bedside lamp. She thought he was going to switch it on, but instead he lifted it from the bedside table and raised it above his head. He was going to crush her skull. She couldn't move. The figure swung the lamp down. Alison closed her eyes and waited for the pain.

. . .

"We crept forward," said Nate. "We didn't know what it was. But we got too close. They didn't want us reporting back. I didn't know why then, but then I met with Colin Trent, and he put together the pieces."

"What did you see?"

"It was a plane. Or at least what was left of a plane. It had probably been burning for hours. But there was a piece of the tail intact. It had either been pulled off in the crash or had been blown away from the wreckage. There was a logo. There were also the remains of its cargo."

"What was the logo?"

"Do you know who Victor Chernenko is?"

"No."

"Neither did I. He's rich. And I am not talking millionaire rich, either. The guy's a billionaire. How he made his money is open to debate. Officially he is an importer and exporter. He has a fleet of large cargo planes picked up for virtually nothing after the Iron Curtain fell. The Russian army wasn't being paid. The generals sold off the armed forces capital, including a handful of Antonov cargo planes. Those things are huge, a building with wings. If you want to get aid somewhere there are no commercial flights, you use someone like Chernenko. These people have a virtual monopoly. They can move anything anywhere - for the right price.

"But the Antonov cargo plane has another advantage. That thing is the fucking Millennium Falcon. There are hidden compartments everywhere. Charities were fuelling the problems they were trying to solve. In order to get aid into a war zone, they would have to use Chernenko. But that would only be part of his payday. The other income would be from the hidden arms in the galley. Rifles, missiles, grenades. Chernenko used to supply both sides. The new armaments allowed the war to continue, meaning that more aid was needed. And of course, there was only one man who could be used. You've heard of a vicious cycle - well, he is the vicious cycle."

"It was his plane?" asked David.

"Condal Air. Spreading death and misery around the world for two decades."

"So if Condal Air is well known for smuggling, what's the big deal of you finding out? Why did they kill your friend?"

"Well, they don't exactly advertise the fact that they are smugglers. That's still illegal. But it was more than that. It was to do with the cargo. I saw them, and so did my best mate."

"Saw what?"

"Tanks."

"Christ, how big was this plane?"

"There were only three tanks. The fire had been so fierce that they had largely burnt up, but I could tell what they were. The route the plane was taking is what's important. They were being sold to a war zone. They were breaching an embargo."

"I thought that was their MO? Okay, they're tanks, but a tank is not going to change the course of a war."

"But a hundred would. This wasn't the first shipment. And you can't just go into a shop and buy a tank off the shelf. Arms sales are regulated. Guns can always get through; they're small and mass produced. They go missing from Army storage, a few hundred here or there. They're shipped to where they're needed and to whoever pays the most. Tanks are different. You can't just drive them out of the back door."

"So if tanks were being smuggled into a war zone…"

"It was by agreement with a body powerful enough to make it happen."

"A country?"

"Most likely. If not someone with great power within a country. Enough power to make everyone look the other way. Either way, tanks are a limited resource. Sooner or later the world is going to find out what has happened and go after the culprit. This wasn't a bid to make money by arming both sides. Someone very important has backed a pony, and they are doing everything they can to ensure their investment pays off."

"Jesus!" exclaimed David, the reality of the situation sinking in. "We have pissed off some very powerful people."

. . .

Spencer opened the front door and looked the person on the other side up and down. She was as advertised, five foot six and blonde. Just like Sally. The call girl was attractive without a doubt - for five hundred pounds an hour, that was to be expected. Yet the differences between her and Sally provided sharp relief to the perfection of the woman he desired. This chattel was a poor copy.

"Hello," said the woman with a faint Eastern European accent.

He had advised the agency that he didn't care what she wore, but the slinky black dress showed that she had made an effort.

It was two o'clock in the morning, and the clock was ticking - and not just on his investment. The room would need to be placed back the way that it had been. Sally could never know he had been here, and that would require time and attention to detail. He wouldn't have time to sleep.

Banner would be in a hotel room across town taking care of business. Spencer knew he should be excited about the nosy bitch getting her comeuppance, but the truth was he was so distracted it didn't give him any joy at all. It was strange. She had looked down on him when they met, that was clear. It was a lesson in not judging a book by its cover. But he just wanted to get it over with; to close this chapter and move on. The next job would be better, less stressful. Victory in this case would just mean that the Russian was not annoyed enough to kill him. Spencer had always thought he was a man who could cope with stress, but the constant prospect of imminent death had not sat well with him. But tomorrow was a new day - a day free of worries and desires.

. . .

He may have been slow to start, but once David had got Nate talking he couldn't stop him. At least now he had some idea why he was going to be killed, although if he was being honest it really didn't make him feel a hell of a lot better. Basically his murder would be down to the fact that some git had got greedy. David was as much a pawn in the game as those at whom the tank guns would be pointed. A whole lot of misery so one man could have a nicer house than everybody else.

Justice needed to find Chernenko. It was a justice that only a few days ago he would have been in a position to provide. Of course, a few days ago he didn't have the information to go public. Now it was too late. They were going to kill him. If he had suspected that before, he knew it now. They had put him in a room with a man who could provide him with the full picture. That would only have happened if there was no chance of him being able to tell the story.

"So how did you end up here?" Asked David.

"Another long story," said Nate. "I ditched the copters in the desert. I had to leave the bike. I ran, and I hid. They swept for hours, but it was dark, and their spotlights could only cover a small portion of the ground. I ran when the light wasn't on me, and soon they were looking in the wrong area. I kept running and then dug in and waited, but they never found me. I guess they ran out of fuel.

"All I know is when the sun rose, I was on my own in the middle of the desert. Great, I thought. I escape the killers and am going to die of exposure. I made my way back to where I thought the road was. I had run farther than I thought; it took me an hour to get back to the road. The sun was hot and getting hotter. And then I saw a truck. It was on the road, maybe half a mile away. Part of me wanted to run - if I had I would be dead now. I didn't run. I waved the truck down. It was an Egyptian driver. The truck was empty, so I guess he had taken supplies to Siwa and was returning home. He drove me all the way back. I so wanted to tell him what had happened, but he didn't speak English. We drove for eight hours in silence. I couldn't imagine what I was going to say to my friend's parents. As it turned out, that wasn't going to be a problem."

"What happened when you got back?"

"I went to the British Embassy. They were waiting for me. I ran. I didn't have a passport. I had ditched it along with my bike. I found the bike on the walk back. It had been torched. My passport and wallet had been taken. I had no money and I couldn't get to the embassy. Then things got really bad."

"How?"

"I saw a TV. There was a news story. It was in Arabic. I didn't understand the language, but I understood the tone. There were two pictures. One of Charlie and one of me. It wasn't a good photo, but it wasn't that I was worried about."

"They were trying to frame you for the murder?"

"Or at least flush me out. Either way, I wasn't going to get to tell my story. So I ran again. I'm good at running. I've spent my life doing it. And suddenly I just wanted to stay still, and I couldn't. I tell you, there is nothing to get you rethinking your life like being hunted."

"Tell me about it. So how did you get back to England? And where have you been staying?"

"I had an old friend that I thought I had lost track of. He owed me nothing, but when I asked he came running and used his contacts and resources to smuggle me back. I had been living in his gaff in North London, as he and his family are in Germany. And then I found Colin Trent. He was a good man. We worked to put it all together. It was going to be all right. I was going to clear my name.

"And then another news story made my world fall apart. Colin Trent was dead. Everyone thought they knew how he died. The poor bastard really didn't deserve that. But they were all wrong. I knew what had happened. And I knew if they could do that to him, I would never be safe. There are people I love. They were so close. But I knew I could never reach out. I could never speak to them. To do so would have put them in danger, and it would have shown those that wanted to kill me exactly where I was. Now it's too late."

TWENTY SEVEN

"So how did they find you?" asked David.

"Wish I knew. I saw them outside, coming up the path, big guys. I managed to get out the back and jump through the neighbour's garden. I just ran and looked for somewhere to hide. I guess I was followed. I used to come here when I was younger. They closed it four years ago now. They were going to turn it into offices, but the funding fell through. I couldn't think of anywhere else to go. I liked it here as a kid. Don't really want to die here, though."

Silence filled the room. David was tired, and now that Nate had finally stopped talking, it seemed a good opportunity to try and sleep. He had all the information he needed, but it didn't affect his situation. He was still a dead man walking.

The chances of getting to sleep were minimal. These would likely be his last hours on the planet, and it seemed a shame to waste them being unconscious. He thought of Alison. He hoped she hadn't followed him. He so wanted not to get her into trouble, yet he knew Alison, and he feared she would keep searching.

. . .

Alison realised she should be dead. The fact that she wasn't was somewhat of a pleasant surprise. She had closed her eyes as the lamp had been brought down. She had expected a sharp pain in her head but instead felt the impact as indirect pressure on her body. Shortly after, the weight was lifted from her chest as a loud thump indicated that her main attacker was now on the floor.

Alison scrambled out of the bed and backed up against the far window. The figure by the side of the bed just stood there. The strange outline of his face was still causing Alison confusion. She shuffled along the window towards the bedside table. Her hand reached for the light switch as she kept her eyes focussed on the figure, ready to react, waiting for a movement that never came. Her fingers found the switch, and the room filled with light. It burned Alison's eyes, although she was less badly affected than the figure in the room, who made a strange sound of pain before ripping something that looked like goggles off his face.

The figure stood there with his eyes closed. Alison could have used the opportunity to attack, but instead she stood and watched. The man was scrawny and pale. He was young. Even with the evidence of the last few minutes in her head, she found that there was something in his face that marked him out as not being a threat. It was gormlessness.

After a couple of seconds, the man opened his eyes. He blinked as the light flooded his retinas. And then he just looked at her. An apologetic smile filled his face.

"Hi," he said.

. . .

Spencer fucked the call girl from behind on top of the sheets that had last been used by Sally. He wore earphones, and as he pumped angrily he listened to a recording of the woman who had bewitched his mind. He thrust hard and fast, and soon he was ready. One final action. Something else he had found in the laundry basket. Underwear. Material that had been close to that place he had dreamed every night of entering. He rubbed the panties into his face, breathed hard through his nose, and came loudly.

. . .

"Hi," said Mattie. He realised it sounded moronic the moment the words came out of his mouth. The problem was there was insufficient social etiquette for how to speak to someone once you had crept into their hotel room and failed to kill them.

Under the circumstances, "hi" seemed like the best of a series of bad options.

"What are you doing here?" asked the woman.

The question was a complex one. It was a question that Mattie had been asking himself the moment they entered the room. Hell, it was a question he had been asking himself for the past few days. When he had watched Banner overpower the woman, it had taken him back. He wanted so much to be the big man. A man that could have taken on Deeko and the Bastard. Now he realised that he had got it wrong. He was on the path to being just like them. He had woken up. He hadn't dropped the light on Banner by accident. It was a fully conscious decision. He had been on the wrong path, and he had acted to turn around, even though in doing so he knew he was putting his life at risk.

. . .

When the call girl had left, Spencer removed the sheets from the bed and replaced them with the originals. Placing the used sheets and covers back in the laundry basket, he kept the knickers in his pocket for later. He had gone through every drawer and surface and compared their position against the photos taken earlier. When he was sure the room was exactly as it was when he arrived, he switched off the light and moved to the living room. Sitting on the sofa, he searched his emotions to see if it had worked. Had he purged her from his system?

He was still trying to work it out when the tears came. And with victory only hours away, Spencer held his head in his hands and sobbed.

TWENTY EIGHT

Banner awoke to find his chest pressed against a two-foot-wide and four-foot-high board. It took him a while to realise that the board was the front of a Corby trouser press. Alison and Mattie had secured his hands inside the press with the belt from one of the two complimentary dressing gowns in the cupboard. They had closed the press so that his hands were sandwiched between the two heating elements. The press was not switched on at the wall - yet.

"Let me out of here, you bitch!" said Banner, his mind finally coming to terms with the situation in which he found himself.

Banner turned and saw Mattie looking down at him. "Did you do this, you retard?"

Mattie smiled at Banner's discomfort. He had never seen him rattled before. He was always so calm. Mattie now knew that the calmness was a factor of control. Now that the control was gone, the guy was bricking it.

"Shut up! We do the talking now," said Alison.

"I am going to kill you," said Banner, his face turning red with rage.

"You tried that. As did some other morons from your outfit. So far you have yet to win a point."

"I am only here because this spastic turned against me."

"Mattie saw the errors of his ways. We spoke while you were unconscious. You were out for a long time. He hit you hard. You are most probably concussed. If you want to throw up, we won't hold it against you."

"Fuck off!"

"Good retort. So, I need some information."

"I'm not saying anything, bitch."

"That's what you think, and I know you believe it, but ask your friends, and they will tell you I have a talent for improvisation and pain. It took you morons to help me realise that, but now I really want to test my skills. We are going to push the boundaries."

"It's a Corby trouser press," said Banner dismissively.

"I always wondered what they were for. Never had a use for one, you see. But now I have. You are going to speak, and if you don't, I am turning on the Corby."

He laughed. "I am going to enjoy myself before I kill you."

"Right. Let's get started, shall we?" said Alison as she moved towards the plug. "Last chance?"

But Banner remained silent. She hit the switch on the wall

and waited for the press to heat up and the screaming to start.

. . .

Spencer was at a crossroads, both metaphorically and literally. The T-junction in front of him had two options: right and left. Right could take him home to his bed, left would take him to her ex-lover. He badly needed sleep. If he was to carry on working for the Russian, he was going to have to renegotiate. The MI5 job would have to go, no matter what the Emissary threatened. The lack of sleep was simply unsustainable. He had expected Banner to take most of the work, but fighting battles on three fronts had left his army too thinly stretched.

Left or right? He would need to go to the stadium tomorrow. There he would arrange the death of the biker and the snooper. He had men camping there, and he was not needed until then. But the chance of meeting the man who had Sally and yet had chosen to leave her behind held an attraction that he couldn't discount. He would never want to meet him in a bar or at a party. Spencer would have had to pretend to be powerless in that situation. That would never do.

But in this moment his power was clear. It was the power to decide life and death. He wanted to hurt this man. It had become personal, but maybe more than that, he wanted to speak to him. He needed some knowledge of why a woman like her would have chosen a loser like the biker. He wanted to know why she still cried for him. To Spencer, it just didn't compute. If he could find the secret, maybe there was a chance for him.

Right was rational. Left was not. Spencer turned left.

TWENTY NINE

The Corby had been on for five minutes but still Banner had not spoken. He didn't even look in discomfort. He was either the toughest man in the world or… Alison reached into the Corby and tentatively touched the plate.

"Is it hot?" asked Mattie, who was sitting on the bed watching the attempted torture.

"It's warm," replied Alison.

"Is it going to get hot?"

"I have no idea how these things work."

Banner laughed at their confusion. "I knew he was a dozy twat, but you are even more incompetent than he is."

"Don't worry," said Alison walking over to the cupboard. "I have a fallback."

She reached inside and pulled out a steam iron. Banner tried to disguise his worry, but he knew the game had changed.

"Mattie," said Alison, "boil the mini kettle. I want to try a range of options."

. . .

David woke up when he heard the rattling of the keys. The door opened, and light flooded in. Standing at the door was the ginger-haired goon and an overweight-looking man in a suit. The suited man looked tired, his tie was crooked, and his collar was yellowing with sweat.

Nate remained sleeping and was snoring lightly on the concrete floor.

The suited man nodded towards Nate.

"Him," said the man.

The ginger goon stepped forwards and grabbed Nate by the collar with one hand. He awoke, a look of shock and fear forming on his face.

"What are you doing?" asked Nate.

But the goon just marched him out of the room, leaving David and the man alone.

David was about to speak, but before he could do so the man turned and walked out of the room. He heard keys jangling, followed by the sound of the lock moving back into place.

David sat alone in the darkness.

. . .

The room was filled with the stench of burning skin. Mattie had to look away towards the end, but just as Alison was about to tip the burning water onto Banner's crotch, the man had finally folded.

He had been tough - at least far tougher than Mattie would have been, and now he was sporting large triangular burn marks across his semi-naked body.

"They're at the Greyhound Stadium," he blurted.

Alison kept the mini kettle tipped. "And David?"

"He's alive."

"Unharmed?"

"He's fine."

"What have they got planned for him?" she asked.

Banner paused, probably trying to work out if he could risk staying quiet. Alison disabused him of the notion by tipping the mini kettle and allowing a glass full of scalding water to pour into his y-fronts. Banner started to scream.

"Scream and you get the rest," said Alison firmly.

Banner squirmed. He bit down against the pain - but remained quiet.

"One more time: What are they going to do with him?"

"They're going to kill him."

. . .

Alison asked Mattie for his phone and dialled a number from memory. Mattie couldn't make out what she was talking about, something about film criticism or some such guff. When she had finished, she passed back the phone.

"What are you going to do?" he asked.

"I am going to get my friend back."

He gaped at her. "You can't just walk in there."

Alison smiled. "I can if I have help on the inside."

THIRTY

Spencer looked at the biker. What kind of a stupid name was Nate, anyway? He had ordered his employees to secure him, and the prisoner was now chained to a sturdy pipe. His feet had been tied with rope, leaving him unable to do anything other than wriggle in place. When Spencer was confident that the biker was incapacitated, he ordered the room to be cleared. Spencer wanted to chat.

He walked over towards Nate. Ordinarily the man would have been a foot taller, but at this moment, Spencer towered over him like a giant. The man named Nate stared back. Intense anger swept over Spencer, and he kicked the biker firmly in the side, then again and again. The biker cried out in pain.

Spencer leaned down. As he did so, he found his hands had automatically formed fists, and before he knew it, he was raining punches down on the man's body and head. Spencer felt as though an outside force were guiding his body. He was out of control, his arms moving without conscious thought. And then the force that was controlling his arms started on his voice.

"Why does she love you? Why does she love you?" he screamed.

Each time he repeated the sentence he threw another punch at the biker's head, but his movements were so wild many of his punches missed their target.

Spencer stepped back. It was only then that he felt the pain in his hands. He looked down to see the blood on his knuckles. The biker was still conscious, but his nose and mouth were bleeding heavily.

Then the controlling force was gone, and Spencer was left alone, looking at the bloodied biker in front of him. He was going to have trouble making it look like an accident now. He had lost control, and that was something a man in charge should never do.

He sat down on the floor, all energy drained.

The two men sat silently and then Spencer spoke. "I used to come here as a kid."

The biker looked back silently.

"My father brought me here. He was a northerner. A miner's son. His father used to take him to the whippet races, and so he brought me here. He moved down before I was born. He wanted me to be something, in the way he never could.

He named me Spencer and taught me to lose my accent. He thought it would make me blend in with those with whom I would need to mix. We are not that dissimilar. Sally isn't for you. She is of the other class. And no matter how hard you try, that is a barrier that can never be crossed."

At the mention of her name, Nate stirred. "You don't go near her."

"She isn't in danger. All I am saying is that you and I are alike. We did everything we could to break into a group that won't accept us. They can smell it on us. Have you ever been whippet racing? Whippets always look terrified. You ever wonder why that is? They run as fast as they can after that rabbit, and when they get there, they realise their goal is fake, worthless. But why are they so terrified? Do you think they see the man that presses the button to open the trap? Do they know of those who bet on them running faster? I don't think they do."

Spencer stared at the man for whom he had been searching for so many days. This wasn't how he thought he would feel at his moment of victory. He should be pitying this man in front of him, but he couldn't. The only pity he felt was for himself.

. . .

The sun had risen by the time Mattie reached the old dog track and the sign with the missing letters bathed in a yellow light. His heart raced as he banged on the gate. After ten seconds, he could see eyes behind staring through at him. The gate opened, and the face of one of the Russian pensioners stared back.

"What you doing here?" asked the Russian.

"Banner ordered me to come over. He's just cleaning up at the hotel."

"The bitch is dead?"

"Very," lied Mattie. "We have the biker?"

"Locked in storeroom," said the Russian before turning back to focus his attention on the fence.

Mattie walked up to the building where a large gateway was open, like the entrance to a modern colosseum. Mattie walked through and into the building. Inside, everything had been stripped away, and only the shell of the structure remained. Through the glassless window, he could see the area that had once been the dog track. A vague impression of the former usage remained, but the grass was overgrown and the concrete cracked and broken.

Mattie guessed that this was where the high rollers would have dined as they watched the races. Across the other side were the simple concrete stands that would have been reserved for the commoners.

There were three men milling about the building. Campbell was standing guard by the side of the door. Shoulders back, arms back - or at least the arm that wasn't broken. Army training never got fully left behind. Looking through the windows, he could see two of the pensioners standing in the centre of the old track.

Mattie now knew where David was, but he was lost on how they were going to get him out of there. The time in the hotel had shown him that Alison was not as feeble as she looked, but these were trained killers, and they were outnumbered. He would have to tell her it was impossible.

Mattie turned and walked back to the entrance. He passed through and back into the exterior area, where the Russian was still looking at the fence. Mattie walked up to him.

"I can take over if you want to rest?"

The Russian looked at him suspiciously.

"I'm pumped up. I'm not going to be able to sleep, but you may be able to."

The Russian weighed the situation and then nodded. He handed a key to Mattie. "I go sleep with others."

"Others?" asked Mattie.

"Everyone is here. Bedroom upstairs. No beds, but there is a room." The Russian smiled and then turned and headed into the building.

Mattie stared at the wall and waited, listening to the Russian's footsteps until they were gone. He waited for another minute and then checked behind. When he was sure he was alone, he put the key into the padlock and turned it until the lock clicked open. Mattie pulled the gate back a fraction and waved his hand outside.

He heard fast-approaching footsteps, and then Alison's face was at the gate.

"Where is he?" she whispered.

"He's locked in a storeroom on the ground floor. But it's impossible. Everyone is here. We're outnumbered ten to one."

"I'm going to get him out. You can help if you want or not. But I am not leaving here without my friend."

"He has a guard posted at the door. The door is locked."

"The guard has a key?" asked Alison.

"I presume so, but he's not going to hand it to you, is he?"

"Then I will have to take it from him."

"He's a trained soldier. A killer. Even if by some miracle you could get the key, there would be ten mercenaries between you and David, and an additional ten killers sleeping upstairs. Any noise and they will be down in a second."

"Then we will have to do it quietly."

"We have no plan."

"Then we'll just have to improvise," she said, staring at him stubbornly. "Now are you going to let me in or not?"

Mattie considered the options. After watching Alison torture Banner at the hotel, he wasn't sure if he was more afraid of her or the twenty killers. He owed her. He had made some lousy decisions, but letting her in would most likely lead to her death. It might be kinder in the long run to…

"Mattie, open the damn gate!"

She had determination in her eyes. He was not going to win this battle.

He pulled the gate aside, and she slipped through. Mattie closed the gate behind her but left the padlock open. If by some miracle they made it out of the stadium, they were going to have to make a speedy exit.

"Right, where's David?"

Mattie pointed to the far-left window. "In a room the other side of that."

"How far is the door from the window?"

"Directly on the other side."

"And the guard's placement?"

"Right in front of the door."

"What are the others in the room doing?"

Mattie shrugged. "Not much. Just sleeping or milling around waiting."

"Tell me about the guard. Who is he?"

"His name is Campbell. He's ex-military. He has a broken arm but is still very tough."

"Will he ever step away from the door? Will he leave his post when he goes to the toilet?"

Mattie shook his head. "He won't move from the door without being relieved."

Alison tried to compose a plan. She looked at the window. The frame was an eight-foot square, with the bottom being six feet off the ground. The glass that would have once sat in the frame was, like the rest of the windows along the wall, gone.

"Whatever you are going to do, you need to do it fast. If anyone comes out to check on me, we're both screwed," said Mattie.

Alison looked at the Jaguar parked inside the fence. She

ran to it and saw the keys were in the ignition. The driver obviously thought it was safe. In fairness to the owner, he did have a private army as security.

"We are going to need a distraction," said Alison, smiling at Mattie.

Without starting the engine, Alison released the handbrake, and they pushed the car along the building until it was below and slightly to the left of the far window.

Pulling the keys from the ignition, she placed them in her pocket. They could come in handy as a weapon.

"Good luck," whispered Alison.

"Wait, what? You want me to distract them? How am I going to do that?" whispered Mattie, a worried look on his face.

"We're both improvising here, remember?"

"Well that's helpful," said Mattie before turning and walking off towards the large entranceway.

Alison placed her palms on the Jaguar's roof and pulled herself slowly up. She tried as hard as she could to be silent, but the roof clunked as the metal gave beneath the pressure of her weight.

She held her breath, but no head appeared at the window. She stood up slowly and placed her back against the wall, with the window frame directly to her left. That had been the easy part. Now she would need a weapon, a real one. She took inspiration from her enemy and how they had killed Colin Trent. She unclipped her belt and pulled it through the hooks of her jeans. Looping it through the buckle, she created a noose.

Now armed, she waited for Mattie's distraction.

THIRTY ONE

Mattie walked through the arched doorway like a gladiator walking towards certain death. He would like to say he had been moved by Alison's faith in his improvisational abilities, but the truth was he had never wanted to be told what to do so much in his life.

Now he was in the building amongst the killers. His eyes searched for something that could be used as a distraction, some object that could activate his terrified mind and move it towards an answer, but he saw no such trigger, and his brain continued to come up blank.

Just as he was about to give up on what was increasingly seeming like a foolish plan, he looked through the glassless windows and saw the answer. Standing there was King Cabbage Muncher. In that second, he knew what to do. He knew the mentality of those around him; he had seen it every day in the hotel. It was the mentality of the school playground. Well, what does the school playground enjoy more than anything else? What was sure to get everyone paying attention?

Mattie walked forwards through a doorway and onto the concrete steps that led down to the track. When he reached the track area, he headed straight towards Cabbage Muncher, who turned towards him and stared.

Mattie kept walking. He didn't slow when he got nearer, just kept moving quickly and with purpose, straight towards his enemy. When he was no more than six feet away, Mattie looked up at Cabbage Muncher, and a big grin filled his face. He took another few steps and without any warning threw a punch straight at his enemy's chin.

He had thrown only a handful of punches in his life, and the results had been largely disappointing. He had never been as big or muscular as the other children his age, which meant that he would usually come off second best. Mattie was therefore surprised when his punch hit its intended mark with strength and purpose. Cabbage Muncher rocked back on his feet, dazed and shocked. For a moment Mattie worried that the fight would be over before it started, but then Cabbage Muncher shook his head and found his feet, at which point Mattie realised he really should be careful what he wished for.

He charged at Cabbage Muncher, but his enemy was now expecting him. Cabbage Muncher threw a heavy punch that glanced off Mattie's head but landed heavily into his shoulder. It was like being hit by a mallet. On previous occasions, Mattie had gone down the moment he knew he was outmatched. But this time he was on the side of right. He was a force for good, and he needed to give Alison time. He threw another punch.

Redemption was going to hurt.

. . .

Alison heard the chatter through the windows. Something was going on, which must mean Mattie had found a distraction.

She paused a moment and then shouted, "Hello up there!"

She waited, hoping that her words would force the guard to look down and lean out to see her. If the guard didn't, the whole plan was shot.

Alison waited. One second, two, three. She was about to speak again, but then she felt a presence by the window. A man's head appeared through the gap in the wall beside her. He didn't see her, his attention instead directed at the ground below.

Alison threw the belt noose around the guard's neck and jumped off the Jaguar's roof. She grasped the belt tightly as gravity took hold. Looking up, she saw the guard's face come to the realisation of what was happening. The belt pulled against her hands, the noose tightened, and Alison heard a loud crack. She landed with both feet on the ground and looked up to the see guard's body fall onto the roof of the car. Fifteen stone of muscle hit the Jaguar's roof with a loud bang, and the roof collapsed a few inches in a vaguely evil guard-shaped dent.

Alison jumped onto the bonnet and moved back onto the roof beside the body. There was no point in checking for a pulse. His neck had snapped - he was dead before he hit the car. Alison reached into the jacket. No key. She tried another pocket, nothing. With increasing panic, she passed her hands over his body. She finally found what she was looking for in his left trouser pocket.

Alison stood upright on the car's roof, her footing less secure now due to the recent heavy denting. She peeked through the window, through to the other side to where a crowd of men stood in a circle. Alison moved quickly and jumped through. Landing on the floor inside, she looked left and right, ready to attack anyone nearby, but she needn't have worried. Everyone was down in the centre of the track.

She looked left and saw the door and knew David was behind it. She ran over, and with shaking hands, she put the key in the lock and turned. She pulled open the door, her heart beating, unsure of what she might find, afraid to make her worst fears true, like a vicious Schrodinger's experiment. When the door opened, she saw David.

The cat was alive.

. . .

David was trying to work out what was going on. He could have sworn he had heard a woman's voice and then a hollow bang, like something hitting a steel drum. Then he heard the key in the lock. He held his breath. Was this his time? He watched the door as it was thrown open to reveal… his best friend. At which point his brain exploded.

Alison ran into the room and threw her arms around him and then, just as quickly released him.

"We have to get out of here!" said Alison.

"Why are you here?" asked David, confusion in every word.

"No time to explain. Can you stand?"

Without waiting for a response, she grabbed his handcuffed arms and pulled him up to his feet.

"There's a guard," he said.

"He's dead."

"How?" asked David, still trying to make sense of the world.

"I killed him. I'm a badass," replied Alison. "Let's go." She dragged him forward, like a hostage being rescued by the SAS.

They got to the door and opened it, and there stood a man known to Alison as Mr Brown in front of them. He seemed surprised to see her.

THIRTY TWO

Spencer left the biker in the room. He had learned nothing. It had been folly. He had no idea why he hated him so much. Now his hands ached, and the pain was getting worse.

He walked back into the main stadium. It took him a moment to work out that no one was around. He heard a commotion to his left and looked onto the track and spotted a crowd of his men. There was something going on in the middle, but he couldn't see what it was. He was about to walk over and lay down the law, but then he turned and saw the storeroom door was open and Campbell was not at his post.

Spencer walked towards the open door as it swung open, and a woman he thought was dead stared back. She seemed as surprised to see him as he was to see her. The woman's arm was supporting the captive. It was an escape attempt. Spencer threw himself at the door, forcing it closed. It pushed back against him before being slammed back closed under his weight. He had physics on his side.

He shouted for the others, but they were so engrossed in whatever they were watching that they didn't look towards him. The door pushed forward again. Spencer shouted once more.

. . .

Mattie's everything hurt. The pain that had started with the blow to his shoulder had increased and spread with every one of Cabbage Muncher's punches and kicks. Mattie was lying on the ground, and it felt very inviting. He wanted to lie there for a while, wanted to make the pain stop. But instead he pushed his body up and, standing on shaky feet, put his fists up once more.

Cabbage Muncher looked at him. To Mattie it looked like something resembling respect, but he may have been wrong. His head had been punched so often he wasn't sure of anything anymore.

"Stop this now," said Cabbage Muncher.

"I'm just getting started," Mattie lied.

But above the ringing in his head, Mattie could hear someone shouting. The crowd in front of him turned and looked towards the main building, to where the Fat Twat was fighting a door. The door seemed to be winning.

The crowd dispersed and ran back to the building,

leaving Mattie on his own. He knew he should escape, but unfortunately his legs had other ideas. His knees crumpled, and he fell back to the ground and promptly threw up.

Just before he passed out, he looked up and saw the door was secure. He knew Alison was still behind it. They had failed.

. . .

Alison felt the door close firmly. She threw her shoulder at it once more, but this time it didn't move. When she heard the lock drop into position, she knew it was over.

Turning to David, who was still trying to come to terms with the reality of the situation, she threw her arms around him.

"I'm sorry," she said.

"What the hell is going on?" asked David. "Hold on. Is this a dream?"

. . .

It took two hours for Banner to escape from the Corby trouser press. He had correctly reckoned that they didn't have the guts to kill him and had been confident that he would break free of his restraints in a matter of seconds once his torturers had left. His plans, however, had to be restructured when the bitch and the runt upended the double bed. They had dragged him and the Corby over to where the bed stood, laid him on his side, and then lowered the bed back over him.

He feared that he would be unable to breathe, but the Corby took enough of the bed's weight to render that fear less urgent than the pain of his burnt chest being pressed against the carpet. It was agony. Worse, the pressure of the bed meant that he was not able to move his arms enough to break free.

Banner had taken a moment to catch his breath. Face down in the carpet, he was breathing in the dust. As a man accustomed to the cleanliness required in barracks, the laziness appalled him. It was a question of pride. He made a note to send an anonymous scathing review to Trip Advisor as soon as he got free, or at least as soon as he had taken care of the bitch and runt.

Banner had used a state of pure fury to ignore the pain and force his way free. Unfortunately for him, he made such a racket escaping that the resident of the neighbouring room had phoned the front desk. The concierge, a man who had spent his life avoiding conflict, awoke a twenty-one-year-old named James Meeker to check out the noise. The concierge attempted to sell the task to the sleepy James as a personal-development objective, but both of them were aware that it was a lie. James wasn't really excited about the prospect of the visit, and it was with trepidation that he prepared to knock at the door to Room 428.

But James Meeker never got the chance to knock, for at that exact moment, the door was flung open, and a large semi-naked man with manic eyes ran past him. Two major things caught James's attention as he watched the man charge away. The first was the large red marks all over the man's body. The second, and at the time more pressing, was that the semi-naked man had a gun. James Meeker didn't know that the gun had no bullets, and it wouldn't have affected his actions even if he did. James believed a gun was a gun, and with this life motto in mind, he ran down to the front desk, picked up a phone and, ignoring the confused-looking concierge, dialled 999.

THIRTY THREE

Spencer had employed an army of Muppets. That was clear now. They had almost let another escape happen. How many people did he have to employ to ensure that unarmed people stayed put in a locked room? He was going to have to restructure, that was for sure. He intended to start now, with the runt, who had said that the woman was dead. The fact that Spencer had just played tug of war with a door meant he had lied. He had told the Russian that Banner was on his way, but he hadn't showed up and wasn't answering his phone. The only conclusion was that the runt had turned.

Spencer led a handful of armed men over to where the runt was lying. There would be no trial. One of these men would get the chance to add another notch on their kill list.

Spencer kicked the runt in the side, but there was no reaction. He thought for a moment that a bullet might not need to be wasted, but when he bent down and placed his fingers on the runt's neck, he could feel a pulse.

He could have ordered the kill there and then, but a large part of him wanted to see the fear in the runt's eyes before the killing bullet was fired. Spencer hated traitors.

He ordered the men to carry the unconscious Mattie back to the building, where they locked him away with the biker.

. . .

Mattie's head was pounding. He looked up to see he was not alone. The other man in the room had a messed-up face. It was a face that looked familiar.

. . .

Alison finally sat down next to David.

"Did you work it out?" he asked.

She nodded. "Smoke and mirrors."

"How long did it take you?"

"Too long. I watched the video over and over. It was there each time. I just didn't put it together."

"In fairness, you never worked as a magician's assistant," he said.

"True. But my best friend was one and bored me about magic tricks enough that I should have got it straight away. When did they catch you?"

303

"I asked questions. I wanted to see if anyone saw the structure the trick would need. It seemed a bit of a long shot, and I didn't think anyone would go to that much effort, but if Colin Trent was murdered, it was the only way it could be done. The environment to make it happen was there. I remembered how difficult it was to find the correct window. It was a modern build, just glass, with nothing to distinguish Trent's window from the one directly opposite. The camera was just looking at that reflection.

"There was an ejection of smoke beforehand. It looked like it was from a machine starting up below."

"But it wasn't, it was a deliberate act to disguise the mirror moving into position. The building was sparsely occupied, meaning the only person that could see the mirror at the precise angle needed was the neighbour, or more specifically, the neighbour's camera. I realised that either the neighbour was in on it or they had scoped out his house and found the camera.

"They used the camera to sell the illusion. They could see the window. Nothing went in or out, except it did. Behind the mirror, they had a crane or suchlike. They may have removed the whole window and just resealed it later. Trent wasn't found for a couple of days, enough time for any sealant to harden. He would have got back to his flat and found men waiting. They killed him with a belt and made it look like it was self-inflicted. After which they moved the window back into position and used another blast of smoke to move the mirror away."

"A long shot," said Alison.

"But a correct one," said David. "It's a very old trick. I used it myself to escape from imprisonment."

"How?"

He smiled. "I'll tell you later."

"There may not be a later."

"Then you will die with a mystery to distract you."

. . .

Spencer had worked out that being clever was not worth the effort. The Trent murder had been a work of art. It was 99% perfect. Unfortunately, the 1% that wasn't perfect had unravelled and caused a mess everywhere, including the roof of his Jag. From now on, it was going to be route one. He was going to have a group execution. They would shoot the four of them in one go, then find some way to dispose of the bodies in a way that they would never be found.

"Who has a silenced weapon?"

Four of the men put their hands up.

"Congratulations. You are the firing squad."

. . .

Alison heard the key turn in the lock and jumped to her feet.

When the door opened, a heavily muscled man stood

waiting.

"I know you are quite tasty," said the man, "but if you strike me down, the guy behind me will shoot you in the tits."

Behind him, an older man had his gun levelled in her direction.

David turned to Alison. "You really have got them worried, haven't you?"

. . .

Spencer watched as his four prisoners were bought out to the centre of the track. This was it, the end of the game. He had won. It had been a tough battle, and one that had lasted far longer than he had expected, but now victory was only moments away. He would be back in the Russian's good books - or at least off the potential death list. Spencer decided that after this, he was going to take a holiday. Maybe he would take up biking.

. . .

Alison and David were dragged to the centre of the stadium. Twenty men had formed a semi-circle, in the middle of which stood four other men with guns. Alison knew those guns would soon be pointing in her direction. She had never wanted to live forever, but she really objected to dying at the hands of these bastards.

Within a few seconds, they were joined by Mattie, along with a man Alison didn't recognise. Of the two of them, it was difficult to say who looked worse. Mattie had obviously been in a fight, and his face looked as if he had lost more severely than any person had ever lost a fight before. The only possible competition he may have had was with the man standing next to him. Maybe they had just put the other person in the line to make Mattie feel better about his appearance. If it wasn't for that, Alison really couldn't work out what he was doing here.

The four of them were lined up next to each other. In front of them, Mr Brown stepped forward. The greasy sod was going to make a speech.

Alison leaned over to Mattie next to her in line. "You okay?" she asked. It was a stupid question, but etiquette had taken over.

"Never better," said Mattie, grimacing in a manner of a man whose face hurt when it moved.

. . .

Spencer was ready to make his speech. He hadn't practiced it, but he had no concerns. He was a natural communicator.

. . .

Alison watched as the weasel she knew as Mr Brown puffed out his chest. He was enjoying the moment, and it pissed her off.

. . .

David was still trying to work out who the suited man was. Alison had referred to him as Mr Brown and she obviously recognised him. He wished for more time on earth, if only to put together all the pieces of the jigsaw.

. . .

Mattie's face really hurt - and now the Fat Twat was going to speak - chuffin brilliant.

THIRTY FOUR

"There won't be a long speech," said Spencer. "There doesn't seem much point in stretching this out. That would be cruel. Be aware, though, that they will never find your bodies. Your friends and family will never know what happened to you."

Alison smiled at him.

"You find this funny?" asked Spencer.

"You really are a sad little fuck, aren't you?" she said.

Spencer was beginning his retort, but then he thought better of it. He turned and walked past the four gunmen, back to the semi-circle of watching men.

"Ready!" shouted Spencer.

The gunmen raised their weapons, pointing them at the targets.

Alison reached her hand out and grabbed David's. He looked towards her and smiled.

"Aim!" shouted Spencer.

Alison reached her other hand out and grasped Mattie's. He looked back at her through swollen eyes.

Spencer took a breath, ready for his final command. But then a terrifying scream echoed across the stadium. The gunmen and spectators turned towards the building to see Banner, naked but for y-fronts, running down the steps, his face, arms, and legs covered in red triangular burn marks.

Banner hit the track, running as fast as he could towards the centre.

"Where are your trousers? And what the hell happened to your face?" asked Spencer.

Banner ran up to the watchers and stopped still. He was breathing heavily.

"I need bullets. Who's got bullets? Sod it, someone just give me a gun."

"What is going on?" asked Spencer. "Are those iron marks?"

One of the mercenaries handed over a pistol. Banner threw his bulletless gun away and grasped the new one.

"That bitch did this," he spat.

Spencer walked towards Banner. "Look, what's going on? Why do you need a gun?" he asked.

Banner weighed the gun in his hand and then quickly pointed it and fired. The shot was loud, the crack echoing around the stadium.

Mattie crumpled to the ground.

· · ·

Mattie hit the ground hard, a feeling he had got used to. The pain in his leg, however, was a whole new experience. He looked down to see a pool of red liquid around his leg. It took him a second to realise that it was blood, and that it was his. Mattie had never been shot, although he had often wondered what it felt like. Now that he had experienced it, he wasn't keen to go through it again. It was a bit of a shame that he was a target of a firing squad, really.

· · ·

Spencer grabbed Banner's arm and pushed the gun away.

"What the hell are you doing?"

"Get your hands off me!" said Banner archly.

Banner shoved Spencer hard in the chest, the impact forcing him to take a step back.

"Are you trying to bring the police here? Silenced weapons only!"

Spencer stepped forward, closing the gap to stand mere inches from Banner. Had he only been a foot taller, he would have been standing face to face with this man. It was an action that at a different time Spencer may have considered reckless, but anger had overcome him. Underlings needed to know their place.

If Spencer was hoping that his right-hand man would take a step back and apologise, he was sadly mistaken.

"That little shit attacked me! He hit me from behind when I was about to kill that bitch. That bitch then did this to me!" shouted Banner.

Banner's anger forced Spencer to quickly recalibrate. He took a step back.

"And we are about to kill them all," said Spencer, attempting calm authority.

"Oh no, those bastards don't get to die quickly. They are going to suffer."

"This isn't about your petty grudges. We're professionals."

"This is the least professional outfit I have ever worked with!" screamed Banner.

Spencer needed his management skills. He recognised there were few guidelines when dealing with professional killers, but the one essential rule was to maintain authority. It was when he wasn't around that everything had gone wrong. It was while unsupervised that his army had let a chained man escape, failed to kill a woman, and almost brought down a plane in hand-to-hand combat. They were vicious fucking idiots.

Spencer needed to reset.

"In that case, you're fired," said Spencer.

Banner laughed coldly. "Fine. Once I have dealt with those two, I am gone. Should only take two or three hours."

Spencer turned to the firing squad. "Fire!" he shouted.

But Banner shouted, "Anyone who fires at those targets will have a bullet in their head a fraction of a second after they pull the trigger."

The firing squad kept their weapons at their side.

"I gave an order!" shouted Spencer.

"Guess you don't have the power you thought you did."

Spencer knew at that moment that power had shifted. Banner smirked. He knew it too.

The argument was cut short by a sound above. They looked up and tried to work out what the hell they were seeing. It was about four feet wide and had four spinning propellers at each corner and was hovering about ten feet above their heads.

And then from behind them they heard the sound of a woman laughing. Spencer turned and looked over at Alison, who was almost jumping up and down with excitement.

"What's so funny?" shouted Spencer.

"Do you know what that is?" asked Alison.

Spencer simply looked at her, his brain was trying to work out his next move, and it was coming up blank.

She continued. "That is a flying spy camera. You can put a heat-seeking camera on it. At the moment it's just carrying a regular camera, and that camera is recording twenty-four pictures a second. Those pictures are being broadcast back to a computer and from there are being livestreamed via a rather pretentious film site. Thereafter the video will be uploaded to YouTube and file-sharing sites for those who were not fortunate enough to see the live broadcast. Wave, Mr Brown, you're on television.

"And whilst it's early in the morning here, it's prime time in Asia and Australia and New Zealand. It's late at night in the States and Canada but they will still be watching. Do you know why, Mr Brown? Because they were waiting for it. You see these are people who get laughed at. They are people always looking for conspiracies. They're deluded people, always searching for and finding patterns where none exist. But let me tell you, when there is a message, no matter how well hidden, they will find it. Because they are magnificent, and that's why people like you will always lose. Because they will always be watching."

And then another voice filled the stadium. It was a voice that echoed louder than any other, for it was being magnified.

"Armed police. Drop your weapons!"

Spencer looked up at the building. Along the glassless windows were twenty police marksmen with guns pointed straight at him.

Spencer looked at Banner with a look that could only be described as terminal frustration.

"You led the police to us, you bloody idiot."

"I said drop your weapons!" boomed the voice.

The private army of Spencer Ignacius Townsend looked up and saw they were outgunned. Spencer heard the sound of weaponry hitting the ground from all around him.

Bloody mercenaries, thought Spencer, they really didn't

have any loyalty.

David looked at Alison. She looked back. He grabbed her, hugged her tight, and before either of them knew it, they were laughing.

"Why do I always have to get you out of trouble?" said David.

The hug ended, and Alison turned her attention to Mattie. There was a lot of blood around his leg, but he was still conscious. She knelt down next to him. "How are you doing?" she asked.

"Everything hurts," said Mattie. "Other than that, I'm not dead, so that's good."

Alison looked up at the other man in the line. She smiled at him. "Er, who are you?" she asked.

"Nate," said Nate.

"Oh," said Alison, no wiser than before she asked the question.

The police were now down from the stand and in the process of securing the mercenaries' hands with zip ties. She watched as the man she knew as Mr Brown had his hands secured behind his back. She nodded at him and smiled. He didn't return the gesture.

And then Alison heard the buzzing above her head. The drone that had been recording everything dropped to eye level and turned its camera towards her. She stood and planted a big air kiss right in front of the camera. And at that moment, a thousand conspiracy theorists fell in love.

They had found their queen.

EPILOGUE

Spencer was feeling good about life. The past four weeks had been tough, but he had survived. The rumoured consequences of bending down in the showers had proven false, and so far both his body and mind had been unmolested. His bespoke garments had been swapped for an orange jumpsuit, but as he had never had a chance to wear his tailored suits, it really didn't bother him that much. What he really liked about prison was the time he now had.

He looked back at the days of working two jobs and wondered how he ever did it. He was an exhausted wreck. How else could he explain how he acted towards Sally? With the distance that prison had given him, he had a chance to see that for what it was - an irrational obsession. He had worked himself to madness. Now that all the things he chased after had been forcibly removed from him, he could see he had been a fool. But his foolish days were over. He knew what was important, and that was him, his mind, and his ability to make the best of a bad situation.

His trial would be in six months, and Spencer looked at his time on remand as an opportunity to get his life together. As he stood on that prison balcony, he looked down at the men on the floor below. They were not so different from the army he had put together, but the beauty of the men below was that he didn't have to manage the morons. Spencer figured that six months would be enough. If the trial went the wrong way, then the six months would be an awful lot longer.

But Spencer had no intention of going to trial. He had cards still to play. He had information for which the authorities would be prepared to bargain. Spencer had been no more than a bit player. He could admit as much - at least when it suited him. There were big fish to catch, and he could offer a sizeable landing net. Spencer knew it was time to get back in the dance. He was convinced he could hear the music.

But as Spencer looked down at the men below, he didn't notice the man walking up behind him. And he didn't notice what was in his hand. For whilst there was a dance, Spencer was not calling the tune. He didn't know it, but he was flailing in the middle of the dance floor as people waltzed around him.

And the dance leader had called time.

. . .

The story broke in a big way, and Alison found herself suddenly famous. The nationals had picked up the story, and while they would have liked to brush over who actually found it, the fact that there was a viral video putting her front and centre made that difficult. The magazine, so close to failure only a few days ago, was now a going concern. More than 100 sponsors had come forward, which meant that Alison and David could finally pay themselves.

When the police had gone to Chernenko's Highgate mansion, there was no one home. The last reported sighting of him was in Russia. The Russian government had so far refused requests to extradite him for questioning. No one knew who he was working for.

With more money in the pot, and the new attention the site was getting, there was an option to take on employees. Alison and David interviewed a handful of media graduates and took on two. They also offered work to two men looking for employment. They knew how they would cope as a target of a firing squad, which could be a useful skill in the work they would do.

One of Enigma Magazine's new employees had instantly proposed to his girlfriend when he returned from their adventure. She didn't say yes, but she hadn't said no yet either, which he maintained was a really good sign.

. . .

Mattie's body was healing, and while he still walked with a limp, life was looking up. He'd never told anyone what had happened when he was in that fight. They knew the details of punches and kicks, but he never said what he saw when he was lying on the floor. Maybe his heart had stopped, or maybe it was just a dream, but to Mattie it had been very real.

His mother had been there. She knew everything he had done, and she knew that the money was gone, but she didn't care. She just threw her arms around his body and hugged him. Mattie remembered the image as though it were real, and for all he knew it was. Maybe she was always watching over him. And if she was watching, then Mattie was going to be good, because he never wanted to disappoint her.

A personal thank you from the author

I am extremely grateful that you have taken the time to travel this far and I hope you enjoyed the journey. Before you go I have a favour to ask. Please take a couple of minutes to post a review on Amazon. This is a first novel and it is jostling for position in a crowded marketplace. Your reviews are the most important factor in this book being able to find its market. It also may give me a chance to feel all warm and fuzzy inside – which is something we all need from time to time.

If you would like to get in touch with me I would be delighted to hear from you. Drop me a message at adrianstclairbentley@hotmail.com or follow me on twitter @AdrianSBentley.

Acknowledgements

Whilst sometimes it's difficult to know where to start a story that certainly isn't the case when it comes to the acknowledgements for this book. My partner, Jéanine Palmer, has been the first set of eyes on everything I have written for many years now. When support is needed she is always there and when a kick up the arse is required it is her boot that delivers it. She also gave me the title (probably).

Many thanks to Annicka Ancliff and Clicia Soares de Lima who gave their feedback on an early draft and allowed me the confidence that I wouldn't be embarrassing myself by publishing this novel.

This book was greatly improved by my editor Crystal Watanabe from Pickko's House.

Expert feedback, of the type that can be paid for with beer, was provided on later drafts by Paul Campbell and Mike Wells. Wellsy also helped by sticking his hand up my rabbit (something that is nowhere near as perverted as it sounds).

Finally my thanks to Tim Courtney for his work on my blurb and for his gentle nagging over this book. In answer to his much-repeated question – "Yes, I've finished it! You can get off my back now!"

About the author

Adrian Bentley lives in London with his partner, Jéanine, their rescue French Bulldog, Mabel, and a robot vacuum cleaner named Sean Spicer.

This is his first novel.

Printed in Great Britain
by Amazon

63546501R00192